12,000 B.C.

The anthropologists of the future had been given a priceless gift—the opportunity to study life nearly fifteen thousand years prior to their own time. Now at last some of the ancient mysteries—that middle area of man's development about which there had been only speculation—could be explored.

But the anthropologists, despite their extraordinary training, were only human themselves. And quickly found themselves subject to the jealousies, fears and other weaknesses to which mankind is subject. Except for one of them . . .

Other titles by Philip José Farmer

INSIDE OUTSIDE

THE ALLEY GOD

THE LOVERS

STRANGE RELATIONS

THE GREEN ODYSSEY

DARE

This is an original publication—not a reprint.

TIME'S LAST GIFT

Philip José Farmer

BALLANTINE BOOKS • NEW YORK
An Intext Publisher

SBN 345-02468-0-095

First Printing: January, 1972

Printed in the United States of America

Cover art by Gene Szafran

BALLANTINE BOOKS, INC.
101 Fifth Avenue, New York, N.Y. 10003

For Lester and Judy del Rey

Chapter 1

The explosion was as loud as a 75-millimeter cannon's.

At one second, there had been nothing but dead wet grass and limestone rocks on the edge of the steep hill.

A gray torpedo shape appeared as if precipitated by some invisible chemical in the air.

The displacement of air caused the boom that rattled down the hillside and the valley and across the distant river and bounced back to the vehicle.

The *H. G. Wells I,* without moving a micron in space, had traveled from A.D., 2070, Spring, to circa 12,000 B.C., Spring.

Immediately after making the long leap in time, it moved in space.

The vehicle had appeared two feet in the air and on the lip of the hill. It fell with a crash to the ground and began rolling.

Forty feet long, its hull of irradiated plastic, it did not suffer from the very steep three-hundred-foot descent. It was not even scratched, though it broke off sharp projections of limestone, and eventually stopped upright at the bottom of the hill after snapping off a score of dwarf pines.

"That was better than the fun-house," Rachel Silverstein said in a quivering voice. She smiled, but her skin was almost as pale as her teeth.

Drummond Silverstein, her husband, grunted. His eyes were wide, and his skin was gray. But the blood was returning swiftly.

Robert von Billmann spoke with a very slight trace of German accent.

"I presume it is safe to unstrap ourselves?"

John Gribardsun twisted some dials on the instrument board before him. A slight whirring told of the projection of a TV camera. The view changed from a blue sky with some high white clouds to dead wet grass ahead and, a mile away, the river at the bottom of the valley.

He turned another dial, and the view switched to the hill down which they had rolled. Halfway up, a fox-like animal jumped out from behind a rock.

The camera swiveled. On the other side of the valley was another animal. Gribardsun turned the closeup dial.

"A hyena," Gribardsun said. His voice was deep and authoritative. "A cave hyena. Looks like a Kenyan hyena except it's much larger and all gray."

Gribardsun had paled only slightly when they had rolled. He spoke with a British accent with a very slight underlying suspicion of another. Von Billmann, the linguist, had never been able to identify it. He had refused to question the Englishman about it because he wanted to label it himself. He prided himself on his ability to recognize any of the major languages and at least two hundred of the minor. But he had no idea of what tongue underlay the Englishman's speech.

The screen showed the view behind the vehicle. A

tiny figure stepped out from the shadow of a huge overhang of rock. It ran to a large rock and dropped behind it.

Rachel said, "That was a man, wasn't it?"

"Has to be," Gribardsun said.

He kept the camera upon the rock, and, after several minutes, a head appeared. He closed up, and
they were looking at a seeming distance of ten feet
into the face of a man. His hair and beard were light
brown, tangled, and long. The face was broad and a
prominent supraorbital ridge shaded eyes of some light
color. The nose was large and aquiline.

"I'm so thrilled," Rachel said. "Our first man! The
first human being. A Magdalenian!"

The man stood up. He was about six feet tall. He
wore a fur vest, fur knee-length pants, and calf-length
fur boots. He carried a short flint-tipped spear and
an *atlatl,* a stick with a notch at one end, which enabled him to cast the spear with greater force. A skin
belt held a skin bag which looked as if it held a small
animal or large bird. The belt also supported a skin
sheath from which protruded a wooden hilt.

Gribardsun looked at a dial. "Outside temperature is
fifty degrees Fahrenheit," he said. "And it's fifteen
minutes past noon, late May—perhaps. Warmer than I
had expected."

"There's very little green as yet," Drummond Silverstein said.

Nobody spoke for a moment. They were just beginning to feel the awe that they had expected to feel.
The transition and the rolling had numbed them, and
the anesthesia of wonder and fright was just beginning
to dissolve.

Gribardsun checked that the equipment was operating
at one hundred per cent efficiency. He ran through
the CAA (checkout-after-arrival), calling out each

item to von Billmann, who sat on his left. The German repeated each, and the words of both were taped. At the end of the checkout, a green light flashed on the panel.

Gribardsun said, "The air outside is pure. It's air that we haven't known for a hundred and fifty years."

"Let's breathe it," Drummond Silverstein said.

The Englishman unstrapped himself and stood up. He was six-foot-three, and the top of his head missed the ceiling by only an inch. He looked as if he were thirty. He had long, straight, very black hair, dark gray eyes, and a handsome, slightly hawkish face. The sheer single-piece tunic revealed a body like Apollo's. He was the M.D. of the expedition, a physical anthropologist, an archeologist, a botanist, and a linguist. If England had not abolished titles, he would have been a duke.

Robert von Billmann stood up a minute later. He was six-foot-two, well-built, thirty-five, titian-haired, and handsome in a pale Baltic way. He was the world's foremost linguist, a cultural anthropologist, an art specialist, and had the equivalent of a master of arts in chemistry.

Rachel Silverstein followed him. She was short, petite, and dark but had light blue eyes. She was long-nosed but pretty. She had Ph.D.'s in genetics and zoology and considerable training in botany and meteorology.

Drummond Silverstein was about six feet tall, thin, and dark. He was a physicist and astronomer and was well trained in geology. He was also a well-known virtuoso on the violin and expert on musicology, preliterate and civilized.

Gribardsun turned the large wheel and pushed open the bank-vault-like port. He stood for a moment in the exit while the others crowded behind him. He breathed deeply and then turned his head to them and smiled slightly.

"I suppose I should say something as poetic as Armstrong's words when he first put foot onto the Moon," he said.

He stepped out onto a narrow strip, the top of a flight of twelve steps, which had slid out when the port was opened. The air was bracing. He sniffed as if he were a great cat, and then he went down the steps. The camera on top of the vehicle had bent over to take in the area of the port because he had set it to track him when he emerged. Its audio was also on. His image and words would be recorded for posterity—if the vehicle returned.

"This is Time's last gift," he said loudly, looking up at the camera. "Modern man will never again be able to travel to this point in time. We, the crew of the *H. G. Wells I,* will do our best to thank Time and Mankind for this great gift."

The others looked disappointed. Evidently they thought that, if they had been given the chance, they could have uttered more notable words.

Gribardsun went back into the vessel and unlocked a box of weapons. Rachel followed him and removed clothes of some light but very warm material which retained body heat very effectively. Armed and weaponed, and two equipped with cameras the shape and size of American footballs, they moved out. The port had been closed, but the camera on top of the vessel tracked them. They began the steep climb with the Englishman at their head. They were in excellent physical condition, but all except Gribardsun were puffing and red-faced by the time they reached the top.

Gribardsun turned and looked back down. The vessel was small. But it weighed three-hundred tons, and it had to be moved back up to the physical point where it had emerged from Time. Otherwise, when the time came to be pulled back to A.D. 2074, the vessel would remain in 12,000 B.C. And so would its crew. The mechanics of time-travel devices required that the vessel, and its original mass within plus or minus ten ounces, be in the exact landing place.

Gribardsun drove a number of sharp plastic spikes into the ground to mark the outlines of the depression formed where the vessel had fallen. Four years from now, the depression might be smoothed out, and thus it would be impossible to locate.

Rachel and von Billmann took films of the spot, and then Gribardsun and Drummond Silverstein took the coordinates of the depression from three large rocks sticking out of the soil nearby.

The *H. G. Wells I* had been set on a wooden platform on top of a hill before being chronologically launched. The edge of the hill in the Vézères River valley, France, A.D. 2070, was forty feet away from the vessel. It had been expected that the edge of the hill in 12,000 B.C. would be even more distant. The geologists had affirmed this to be a fact. Gribardsun wondered if they had been correct but a slight displacement in space had occurred. The theoreticians said that this would not occur, but the truth was that they did not know what would happen in practice.

The process of time travel required an enormous amount of energy. The further back into time the machine went, the more the energy. This period was as far back as a machine could be sent. There was a factor, which only a few mathematicians understood, which required that the most expensive and most dangerous journey be made first. If the time travelers waited, say, eight years more before attempting to go into the Magdalenian, they would find themselves in circa 8000 B.C. The era of 12,000 B.C. would be forever out of reach. And if they waited for ten years, they would find that 4000 B.C. was as far back as they could go.

Moreover, there was a strange and unexplained limit at the other end. The first small experimental manless model had been sent back one day into time. But it had never arrived, as they knew it would not, having been present the day before. Where the model went was not known. Then another model, at great expense of materials and energy, was sent back a week. This did not appear, as the experimenters knew it would not. But they had to be sure.

At this time, the news media learned about Project Chronos, and it was suspended for a while until the public, and Congress, were satisfied that it was safe. The old science-fiction idea that tampering with time would change the course of events had to be dealt with. Stories by various writers from Wells to Silverberg and Bradbury and Heinlein, illustrating the paradox and danger of time travel, were reprinted and even dramatized. Millions of people were fearful that time travel would result in one of their ancestors being killed, and so their descendants would vanish from the face of Earth, as if the boojum were prowling it.

Jacob Moishe, leader of the project team that had invented the time-travel machines, quieted this form of protest. He showed, in a series of articles, that if time travel was going to make any changes, it had already done so, and therefore there was nothing to fear. By then the original goal of circa 25,000 B.C. was lost forever. Too much time had elapsed. The expedition would have to settle for the middle Magdalenian. The funds were restored, and a small model was sent back to one hundred years, and a search was made for it. The theory was that it had appeared in A.D. 1973 and had been picked up by someone who did not, of course, recognize it. But, since it was practically indestructible, it existed now and was probably in someone's possession. Or perhaps buried some place. Worldwide advertising failed to turn up the model.

Meanwhile, another had been sent to A.D. 1875, and the advertising for this one went around the world. None showed up. A third one was sent back at a cost that staggered Congress and the public. This one was set to bob up about A.D. 1850 within fifty feet of where the project buildings stood.

Dr. Moishe's researches had shown that, in 1850, this hilltop in Syracuse, New York, had been the scene of a mysterious and exceedingly violent explosion. He reasoned that the explosion had been caused when the model had appeared inside some solid matter, such as soil or a tree; the result of two solid objects trying to occupy the same space had been the explosion. A complete conversion of matter to energy had not occurred, of course. Otherwise, the hill and much of the surrounding countryside would have disappeared.

The model contained radioactive particles, and so, after it was sent back to 1850, the area for a mile around was scanned with geiger counters. A piece of the radioactive particle-bearing model was located and identified. Accusations of fraud were, of course, made, but Dr. Moishe had foreseen this and made foolproof arrangements. He had even gotten six congressmen and the Secretary of Science to watch the entire procedure.

One of the theories about the failure of the first two models to be found was immediately dismissed. This theory postulated that the structure of time was such that time travel was impossible within any period in which contemporaries had been living. In other words, time, to avoid a paradox, but not the pathetic fallacy, would not permit travel except in a time before anybody living in A.D. 2070 had been born. The critics pointed out, none too gently, that this would mean that somebody born before A.D. 1875 was still living and that his presence was keeping the models from appearing in A.D. 1973 and 1890. If the hypothetical person was born in, say, A.D. 1870, then he would today be 200 years old. And that was impossible, for several reasons. For one thing, a record existed of the birth date of everybody living, and the oldest person in the world was 130. She had been born in A.D. 1940.

The theory was admittedly farfetched, if not crackpotted. Its proponent, who later committed suicide for unknown reasons, and so discredited any reputation he had for sanity, replied that anyone that old might have some reason for not wanting to be known. And it was not impossible to fake records.

John Gribardsun was thinking of this when Rachel Silverstein touched his arm. She seemed to be touching him at least ten times a day, as if she were testing to make sure that he existed. Or because she liked to touch him. He did not mind it, though he knew that Drummond disliked it. But it was up to her husband to say something about it to her, and, so far as he knew, the man had never opened his mouth about it.

"Do you think we can get the ship back up by ourselves?" she said. Her light blue eyes were bright, as if she were burning with excitement.

"I suppose so," he said. "But I think we could do it far more swiftly and easily if we had the strong backs of some cavemen helping us. So we won't worry about it now. After all, we have four years."

Robert von Billmann said something sharply. He was looking through binoculars to the northeast, across the valley. Gribardsun saw the figures that had attracted von Billmann. He lifted his own binoculars. The heads and antlers of several brownish reindeer came into view. He moved the glasses and within a minute had zeroed in on a big grayish shape. It was a wolf. Soon, he caught about a dozen with a sweep of the glasses.

The deer were well aware of the wolves. They continued to crop at the moss between liftings of the head, to sniff the air, and to eye the slinking beasts some fifty yards distant.

Presently some of the gray shapes floated behind a hill and soon appeared ahead of the herd. They disappeared again, and then those that had remained moved in slowly toward the herd. The deer waited for a minute to make sure that the wolves would not stop and suddenly, as if the leader had spoken, they bounded away. The wolves ran after them, and then, as the herd passed the hill behind which the others were, they veered away. Six wolves had run out at them. One wolf caught a doe that stumbled, and the others leaped upon it. The remaining deer got away, except for a buck that slipped when he leaped across a brook. Before he could get up again, he found two wolves tearing at his legs. These were joined by others, and the wolves quit running.

Gribardsun had been watching with keen interest. He put the binoculars down and said, "And to think that the only wolves in our time were in zoos or small reservations. These beasts have a whole world to roam in. And there must be millions of them."

"Sometimes I think you're the zoologist," Rachel said.

"I am a naturalist."

He turned and looked down the valley where they had seen the man. He had long ago hidden behind a rock and, though Gribardsun had stopped on the way up the hill to search for him with his binoculars, he had failed to find him. Now the man, having seen the four leave the vessel, was approaching it.

"Curiosity kills more than a cat," Gribardsun said.

The man's home might be a little way off or many miles. The expedition had quite a few daylight hours left, so they might as well take advantage of it. There was much work to do.

He allowed the others to collect their samples of soil, plants, and rocks and to take some more photographs. Then he said that they should return to the vessel, store their samples, pick up food and trinkets, and set out up the valley to look for a human habitation.

They started back down the slope. The man was within a hundred yards of the great torpedo shape. Seeing the four coming down the hill, he ducked behind a boulder. He remained there until Gribardsun opened the port of the vessel. Then he rose and, bending over, ran to a more distant rock. Drummond Silverstein took some more films of him.

They packed their bags and strapped them onto their backs. Gribardsun took the .500-caliber express rifle. Von Billmann and Drummond carried the rifles which shot anesthetic darts. Rachel carried a .30-caliber automatic rifle. Each had an automatic pistol in the holster at his belt, and they had explosive and gas grenades in their sacks.

They started up the valley and presently came to a small stream which meandered down to the river below. They followed along the stream for a time. The man kept ahead of them by a quarter of a mile.

At the end of two miles, they decided to climb up through the base of the cliffs. There were some overhangs that looked interesting. These turned out to have been inhabited by men, judging from the rude hearths of stone, the bones, flint and chert fragments, and pieces of wood and fur. A half mile on, they found a narrow cave which stank as if hyenas had once lived there. Rachel said that she would study it later and determine what hyenas ate and so forth. She threw some rocks into the interior but got no result.

They walked five miles before they came to the man's home. The valley suddenly widened here, and the overhang which housed human beings was at the top of a steep slope. They could not see any women or children from this angle, but the twelve men would not have gathered in full sight on the edge of the hill unless they had something to defend.

Gribardsun looked around before giving the order to ascend. It seemed likely that there would be other men out hunting, and he did not want to be surprised by men attacking from behind.

The man they had first seen had scrambled up ahead of them to warn the others. Now he stood with the others, brandishing his spear and yelling at the invaders.

Gribardsun activated the bullhorn device on his chest and then told the others to drop about a hundred feet behind him. He looked for large rocks on the lip of the hill. He was ready to jump if they rolled any down on them. But there did not seem to be any nor was there evidence at the foot of the hill that they had rolled any down in the past.

He wondered what the natives were thinking. There were twelve warriors there, defending their home territory, and there were only three men and a woman boldly approaching them. Their appearance, of course, would be impressive. There would be something very alien about the invaders; the clothes, the weird-looking weapons, the clean-shaven faces. Most mystifying, and terrifying, would be the confidence with which the greatly outnumbered party approached.

Gribardsun had had long experience with savages. He was much older than he looked and remembered when Africa and Asia still hid genuine preliterates with very little knowledge of civilization. It was this experience which gave him confidence, because he knew that these people did not really want to engage in combat with an unknown enemy. The others of his party had had little to do with genuine primitives; they had been born too late; the savages had died out or been citified; the few left on reservations were too well-educated to be "real" primitives.

Nevertheless, the natives were dangerous. They must have fought enemy humans and they must have hunted the dangerous mammoth, rhinoceros, cave bear and cave lion.

Gribardsun got well within range of the spears before he held up his hand for the others to stop. He advanced slowly then, speaking through the bullhorn. His voice, like a thunder god's, bellowed at them. They stopped yelling and waving their weapons when the first words struck them. Even at this distance he could see their flushed skins turn pale.

He stopped, too, and pulled out a Very gun and fired it straight up into the air. The parachute expanded from the stick, at two hundred feet, and as it fell it burned a bright green and then a bright scarlet and then exploded loudly at a fifty-foot altitude.

The warriors became rigid and silent.

They must have wanted to run, but that would have meant abandoning the women and children. And that they would not do.

Gribardsun approved of this. Though they must have felt a terrible awe of this evil magician, yet they stood their ground.

The Englishman held out both hands—his express rifle was still supported by a strap over his shoulder—and he advanced smiling.

A tall heavily built man with dark red hair mingled with gray stepped out of the line and approached Gribardsun slowly. The brown-haired man whom the party had followed also came down the slope though he stayed a few feet behind the red-haired man. The chief held a big stone axe in his right hand and a thick-shafted spear in his left. He was about as tall as Gribardsun.

The Englishman spoke through the bullhorn again. At the thundering speech, the chief and his companion stopped. But Gribardsun continued to smile, and then he turned the amplifier off, lowering his hand slowly so he would not alarm the two. After that, he raised his hand and spoke with his normal voice. The eyes of the two widened at this. However, they seemed to understand that the change in loudness was meant to signify friendliness.

Gribardsun walked slowly upward until he was about ten feet from them. At this range, he could see that both were quivering. But it was the alienness of the intruders that was making them shake, not the prospect of combat.

Gribardsun talked and at the same time made signs to reinforce the words. He used the sign language of the Kalahari bushmen, not because he expected the sign language of these people—if they had any—to coincide but because the signs would be additional reassurances of his peaceful intentions.

He told them that the four came from a far place and that they brought gifts and that they were friends.

The chief finally smiled and lowered his weapons, though he still kept his distance. The other man also smiled. The chief turned, still watching Gribardsun out of the corner of his eyes, and shouted at the warriors above. Then he beckoned Gribardsun to follow him, and he and the brown-haired man preceded the four. At the top they found themselves ringed by the warriors but these made no threatening gestures.

The four could now see that there was a large camp under the immense limestone overhang. The north end was blocked by stones piled on top of each other and part of the eastern end was also blocked. There were about thirty "wigwams," tents of skin supported by wooden poles, near the rear of the overhang. Gribardsun counted thirty adult women, ten juvenile girls, six juvenile males, and thirty-eight children. Later, when hunters returned, the total adult male population would be twenty-four.

There were small fires in every hearth and wooden spits over many, some of which held skinned and gutted rabbits, marmots, birds and parts of a bear. In one corner was a wooden cage in which was a bear cub. Before one of the tents was a pole held up by a pile of rocks and dirt. Stuck on its end was a bear skull easily as large as the largest of the Kodiak bears of Gribardsun's time. Gribardsun wondered if the skull and the cub meant that the tribe had a bear cult.

Water would have to be brought up from the river. A number of skin bags on the dirt floor seemed to hold water.

There were bones all over the place, and a strong odor from the north indicated that human excrement was dropped over the edge of the hill on the other side of the rude wall. The odor of the natives, and their matted hair and beards and dirty skins, showed that they cared little for personal cleanliness.

Gribardsun walked over to the nearest tent and looked inside without objection from anybody. There were very low beds with wooden frames and furs piled on top. On one lay a boy of about ten. He stank of sickness.

Gribardsun crawled into the tent after telling Rachel to hold the skin flap open for him. The boy looked at him with glazed eyes. He was too sick to be frightened by the stranger.

A woman shouted something outside and then crawled in to watch the stranger. She was making sure that the mysterious man with the voice like thunder did not intend to harm her child.

Gribardsun smiled at her but also made a gesture for her not to interfere.

He put a reflector on his head and shone a light into the boy's eyes and down his throat and into his ears. The boy submitted though he trembled with fear.

Gribardsun had to decide whether or not to take samples of skin tissue, blood, saliva and urine. So many of the preliterate societies he had known had objected to giving specimens. They feared that these would be used against them by evil magic. If this tribe had the same superstitions, it might react violently, no matter how awed they were at this moment.

He considered. The flat instrument he had applied to the boy's skin indicated a fever of 104° Fahrenheit. The skin was flushed and dry. The breath was foul. The heartbeat was eighty-five per minute. The breathing was rapid and shallow. These symptoms could mean a dozen different diseases. He needed specimens for a diagnosis.

He could just back off and let nature, or whatever the local witch doctor might have in the way of efficacious medicine, do its work. He had been warned that he should not get involved with medical matters if he thought that his interference might backfire. After all, everybody he would meet was doomed to die, would have been dead for almost fourteen thousand years when he was born. But procedure was left to his discretion. If he thought he could cure a sick native, and thereby aid the goal of the project, he could proceed. But if he did not wish to endanger the project, he could just let the natives die.

There was no question or concern about his interference changing the course of events. Whatever he was to do had been done, and events and lives had been determined before he was born even if he had helped determine them.

Gribardsun's back kept the mother from seeing what he was doing. She said something in a protesting tone, but he paid no attention. He stuck the tip of the instrument against the arm, twisted a little knob on its side, and the syringe filled with blood. He drew off some saliva from the boy's open mouth. Getting urine would be difficult only if the mother objected. He secured another instrument at the proper place, and pressed a button plunger on the end of a flexible metal tube. If there was any urine available, it would come out without delay, and it did. He removed the instrument and packed it away. When he returned to the vessel, he would make his analyses. Rather, the small medical computer in the ship would. And tomorrow, if things went right here today, he would transport the computer-analyzer to this site.

The mother protested some more, but she crawled out of the tent a moment later. Perhaps she was going to the chief and the medicine man. He took advantage of her absence to drop a pill into the boy's mouth, raise his head, and pour ill-smelling water into his mouth from a skin bag.

The pill was a general panacea—a redundancy in terms—which could slow down the development of a dozen diseases. It might not contain anything to help whatever was making the boy sick, but there was nothing in it to hurt him.

Outside, the woman was talking rapidly and loudly and gesticulating to the chief and a short muscular man with a forehead covered with symbols painted with ocher. The symbols matched those on the skin of the tent. This man had just come in from the hunt. His woman was carrying off two rabbits and a large badger.

Two more men climbed over the edge of the hill. One, a huge man with the massive muscles and the potbelly of a gorilla, was carrying part of a large male reindeer over his shoulders. The other, shorter and less stout, was carrying the smaller portion over his shoulders and a marmot tied by the neck to his belt.

The two stopped when they saw the strangers. The carcass dropped with a thump and a clash of antlers against a hearth, and the giant advanced toward them. The chief said something to him, and the giant stopped, scowling.

The first thing to do was to establish "identities." Gribardsun got them to pronounce—or try to pronounce—their names. They did better with John than with his surname.

The chief was Thammash. The brown-haired man was Shivkaet, the tribal artist. The painted man was Glamug, the witch doctor or shaman. The giant was Angrogrim. The sick boy was Abinal, son of Dubhab. Dubhab showed up during the name-learning. He was a short lean man with a wide friendly smile, and he seemed to be the most articulate of his people. He introduced others, including Leminak, his daughter, a preteenager, and Amaga, his wife.

Gribardsun told his colleagues it was time to go back to the vessel. They would not stay too long today. Despite their violence-free reception, they were putting the natives to a strain. They would retreat and let the tribe discuss the strangers. Tomorrow they would return and stay a little longer. And the day after they would increase the length of their visit even more. In time, the natives would get used to them.

Von Billmann said, "I can hardly wait to study their language. Did you catch that synchronic articulation of the nasal bilabial and the velar bilabial and the ejective consonants with simultaneous glottal stops?"

"I caught them," Gribardsun said.

Rachel rolled her large blue eyes and said, "I think I'm going to have trouble speaking their language anywhere near correctly. The sounds sound impossible."

Drummond said, "Robert, you look as excited as if you were about to make love."

"Which he is, in a way," Gribardsun said.

They left, while the tribe gathered on the edge of the hill to watch them. Some of the small boys started down after them but were called back by their parents. The people stood together and watched them until they were out of sight.

They were not very talkative on the way back. Von Billmann had stuck the speaker of his pocket recorder-player into his ear and was listening to the sound of the language over and over. Rachel and Drummond spoke infrequently and then softly to each other. Gribardsun seldom talked much unless the occasion demanded it.

However, when they returned to the *H. G. Wells I,* their spirits rose. Perhaps it was because they were home. Even the grim gray torpedo shape was a haven and reminder of the world they had left.

"We'll sleep here tonight," Gribardsun said. "We can put up our domes later on. Obviously we can't walk back and forth to the village every day, and we can't move the vessel, so we'll have to establish camp close to our subjects."

Rachel busied herself getting supper, though this took only two minutes to cook and open the prepared packages. She did pour out small glasses of wine to celebrate. Gribardsun ran the specimens through the analyzer while she was getting supper.

"The boy, Abinal, has typhus," he said. "That can be caused by a rickettsia or body lice. I didn't see anybody else sick, so I doubt that it was caused by body lice, though Abinal may just be the first. Whatever the cause, he can transmit it through his own body lice. I propose tomorrow to give Abinal an antityphus medicine and to give the others a preventative. Plus a medicine which will kill their body lice."

"How do you propose to get them to take the medicines?" von Billmann said.

"I don't know yet."

"It might cause more trouble than it's worth," Drummond said. "Not that I'm ignoring the human side of this," he added, seeing Rachel's frown. "But, after all, we want to study them in their natural habitat and in their natural mode of life as much as possible. If we prevent diseases, how will we know how they react to them? I mean, what medicines and magical rituals they use, their burial ceremonies and so forth. You know they're going to die anyway—in fact, they've been dead for a long time, actually. And what kind of resentments will you stir up if you interfere with the shaman's profession or fail to cure a sick person? You might even get blamed for the death."

"That's true," Gribardsun said. "But if the tribe is wiped out by typhus, or some other disease, then we have no tribe to study, no language to learn. And nobody to help us haul the vessel to the top of the hill. I'm taking what they used to call a calculated risk."

Rachel looked curiously at him and said, "Every once in a while you use an old-fashioned phrase. Not self-consciously but as if—well, I don't know. You roll them out as if you were to the phrase born, if you know what I mean."

"I read a lot," he said. "And I have a tendency to repeat some of the good old phrases."

"I'm not deprecating it," she said. "I like to hear them. It's just that they startle me. Anyway, supper's on. Let's have a little toast first. John, you're our chief; you propose it."

He raised his glass and said, "Here's to the world we love, whatever she may be."

They drank down the wine. Rachel said, "That's a strange toast, John."

"John's a strange man," Drummond said, and he laughed.

Gribardsun smiled slightly. He knew that Silverstein resented his wife's obvious admiration for him, but he did not think that the issue would be an irritating one, even if they were forced to be together for four years. The scientists in charge of the project had studied their compatibility charts and were well satisfied with them. Nobody on the expedition was psychologically unstable, as far as the tests could determine.

If Drummond got out of line, he would have to be straightened out. He was a reasonable man, except where his wife was concerned. And even there he could be reassured. Gribardsun was sure of that. It was only in the last few weeks before the launching of the *H. G. Wells I* that Drummond had started to show signs that he thought his wife admired Gribardsun more than she should. Even then he had expressed himself in only mild oblique remarks. Several mornings, he and Rachel had looked as if they had not slept well the night before. Gribardsun had thought of asking for their withdrawal before the day of launching got too close. But the two had not let whatever was bothering them interfere with their duties, and he knew how deeply they would be hurt if they were taken off the project. So he had said nothing to his superiors.

"We'll get up early," he said. "Seven o'clock, ship's time. After breakfast we'll tramp around and collect some more specimens. Then we'll visit our natives. But I think we can establish even better relations if we take them some meat."

After eating, they went outside. The sun was just touching the horizon. The air was very cold. A herd of about thirty reindeer, a couple of huge rhinoceroses, twelve adult mammoths and three babies, and a dozen bison were by the river. At this distance they looked like small animated toys.

The four were thrilled at their first sight of the rhinos and mammoths. There were still elephants in zoos and reservations in their world, but the mammoths with the hump of fat on their heads and shoulders and the curved tusks were quite different. And the rhinos were extinct in the twenty-first century.

"There're some wolves!" Rachel said.

She pointed, and they saw about a dozen of the gray shapes floating out of the shadows of a hill. The reindeer raised their heads, and the faint trumpeting of the mammoths reached the four. But the wolves ignored them and trotted to a spot about sixty yards down from the herbivores. There they drank, and the herbivores continued to drink, though watching the wolves nervously.

The sky above passed from pale blue to dark blue to sable. The stars came out. Drummond Silverstein made sightings, then set out his telescope and camera. Rachel stayed out with him. Von Billmann returned to the vessel to listen some more to the sounds of his new language. Gribardsun took his express rifle and walked back up the hill. By the time he reached the top, the half moon had appeared. It looked exactly

like the moon he knew, except that he knew that no
men were burrowed deep in its rock and no domes
or spacecraft were on its surface.

He faced the wind, which was blowing at about six
miles an hour from the northwest. It also brought
sounds: from far off a lion's roar; nearer, a small cat's
scream; the snorting of some large beast, rhino or
bison; the clatter of hoofs on rocks to the west. The
lion roared again and then was silent. He smiled. It
had been a long time since he had heard a lion roaring.
This one was deeper than any he had known; the cave
lion was somewhat larger than the African.

A mammoth trumpeted shrilly from near where the
lion's roar had come. Then there was silence.

After a while he heard a fox bark. He lingered
a few more moments, drinking in the rising moon
and the pure air, and then he returned to the ship
below. Drummond Silverstein was putting away his astronomical equipment. Rachel had gone.

"I like this world already," Gribardsun said. "I knew
I would. It's simple and savage and uncrowded with
humans."

"Next you'll be saying you want to stay behind
when we leave," Silverstein said.

He sounded as if he did not altogether disapprove
of the idea.

"Well, if a man wants to know this time thoroug-
ly, he'll have to stay here the rest of his life," Gribardsun said. "He could explore Europe and then cross
the land bridge to Africa. As I understand it, the Sahara is a green and wet land with rivers full of hippos.
And the sub-Sahara, my old stamping ground, is a
paradise of animal life. And there might even be a
few subhumans left, roaming the savannahs or the
forests."

"That would be self-indulgent and suicidal," Drummond said. "Who would gain anything from it? All that data and no one to leave it to."

"I could leave a record of some sort at an agreed-upon place, and you could pick it up immediately on returning," Gribardsun said. He laughed, then picked up a large plastic box containing recording equipment and followed Silverstein into the vessel.

"You talk like von Billmann," Silverstein said. "He's grumbling already because he won't get a chance to locate and record pre-Indo-Hittite speech. He's talking of making a trip by himself to Germany."

"There's nothing wrong with dreaming," Gribardsun said. "But we're all scientists and thoroughly disciplined. We'll do our job and then go home."

"I hope so," Drummond said as he stowed away his equipment in the middle cabin. "But don't you feel something in the air? Something . . . ?"

"Wild and free?" Rachel said. She was looking at Gribardsun with a peculiarly intent expression. "The soul of the primitive is floating on the air."

"Very poetic," von Billmann said. "Yes, I feel it too. I think it's because we've been living in a cramped and regulated world, and suddenly we're released with a whole unspoiled world to ourselves, and we feel like exploding. It's a psychological reaction that our psychologists didn't foresee."

Gribardsun did not comment. He was thinking that if this were true, then those who originally were the wildest and had repressed the most, would react the most violently.

The Silversteins let down their wall bunks in the middle room and closed the port after saying good night. The other two went to bed. The vessel was not spacious, but it was designed to be lived in for four years if the explorers found it necessary.

Gribardsun's ear alarm went off at five A.M., ship's

time. He rolled out and did a few sitting-up exercises, ate breakfast, put on clothes, and left. He carried an express rifle in one gloved hand and a short-range rifle which shot anesthetic missiles in a sheath over one shoulder. He also carried a big hunting knife and an automatic pistol.

The air was cold and pale. The sun had not yet risen, but it was bright enough to see everything clearly. His breath steamed. He climbed briskly despite the weight of sack and weapons. His clothing was thin and light but very warm. After a while he had to unzip the front of the one-piece suit to cool off.

At the top he stopped to look back. He had left a message for them in the recorder-player. He might be back before they awakened.

He turned and trotted away down the gentle slope. He was exuberant. This was a wild land, not nearly as vegetation-grown as he would have liked it, but the open stretches had an appeal.

He had gone perhaps a mile, still trotting, when he flushed out grouse from a stand of dwarf pines. A minute later he saw a brownish fox scud from a ravine and across a field to a hiding place behind a boulder. Half a mile farther on, he had to swing northward because of six woolly rhinoceroses, one of which made short savage charges toward him.

He kept on trotting. The sun rose, but not for long. Clouds appeared and covered the sky quickly. And half an hour later, rain fell heavily.

His clothing was waterproof. But the water was cold and chilled his face. He passed a herd of vast shapes with humped heads and necks and great curving tusks. They were plucking up moss and the large flat cushions of a plant with white flowers (*Dryas octopetala* probably), saxifrage, and the dwarf azaleas, willows and birch. He could hear the rumbling of their stomachs above the downpour. It was an old sound and a soothing one. He felt at home despite the freezing rain.

A little later he came to stands of dwarf pines again. As the glaciers retreated northward, the pines would appear in growing numbers. South, in lower Iberia, taller pines would be spreading over the land.

Gribardsun had been following the edge of the top of the valley. When he was above where he estimated the natives were, he looked over the edge. He had stopped almost exactly above them. The overhang, of course, hid their dwelling place, but he recognized the hill and the land below it. There was no sign of life. Either the hunters were staying home because of the rain, which did not seem likely since they had not been overstocked with meat, or they had already left. He resumed his trot but turned northward again, intending to make a circle and return to the vessel. He would be late, but that did not matter. They had their work to do first, and they could still start out for the site on schedule. He wasn't worried about the boy, Abinal. The panacea he had given him worked against typhus. Its effect would last for several more hours.

The rain was as heavy as before. He splashed along for a while and then decided to cut straight back to the vessel. The rain had discouraged most beasts from coming out.

He turned to the west and started back up the long slope. As he passed by a high outcrop of limestone, he slowed down. If he poked around in there, he might scare something out. He stopped and removed his small motion-picture camera from the bag and took some shots. Then he went up to a gap between two tall rocks and threw several stones into it. Something grunted from deep within. He back away and pointed the camera at the opening. Nothing, however, emerged.

He threw some more stones inside, heard another grunt, and entered the gap. He did not know what was inside. There were no tracks since stone covered the entranceway and the rain would, in any event, have washed away odors. When he got about twelve feet inside the gap, however, he smelled bear. He had installed the camera inside his hood; its base was secured to a helmet-like arrangement which fitted around his head and which he had removed from the pack. Thus, he could take pictures and at the same time handle his express rifle. If the light was too dim to give good pictures, he could always erase the electronic film.

He did not intend to kill the beast. He never killed unless he had to do so for defense or meat. But he had been so long without adventure that he could not resist sticking his head into the den. Later, he admitted to himself that he had lost his good sense for a moment. What did he expect a bear on its home territory to do other than charge the trespasser?

The beast heard or smelled him, and it snarled. He went on, his rifle held out ahead of him. The gap curved to the left for about ten feet and then straightened out. It had narrowed overhead to a thin line and then, within a few feet, its edges merged.

About that time, either his wits returned or his blood cooled. He was not afraid, but he did not want to kill the bear. What good would it do anybody? Then it occurred to him that the meat would not spoil. The people would walk through the rain to get it, even if it was about five miles away. He could block up the entrance with rocks to keep the hyenas and wolves away. And this morning's indulgence (that was what it was) could be justified.

Of course, he could have killed a mammoth or rhino

but then the carcass would have been out in the open and so subject to the carrion eaters.

He grimaced. He did not have to justify himself to anybody except himself.

The snarling became a roaring, and a huge head with white-edged eyes and dripping saliva showed itself a few feet ahead of him. The gap was so narrow that the great beast had to shove both shoulders against the walls to get through. Gribardsun fired the rifle; the noise was deafening in the tight corridor; the .500 express bullet went through the skull between the eyes and the beast fell dead.

Another bear behind it, roaring, tried to get at Gribardsun by climbing over the carcass. It became stuck in the narrower opening higher up, and Gribardsun's bullet went into its throat. It died on top of its mate.

The Englishman climbed over the top body and into the dark and fetid chamber. He turned on a flashlight and inspected the cave. As he had expected, there were two cubs. They cowered in the rear but snarled at him when he picked them up. He threw them ahead of him over the bodies, climbed out again, and then had to chase them down. He had expected them to stay close to the bodies of their parents, but they wanted their freedom.

After catching the cubs, he injected a *dormgen* shot into each. While they snoozed away, he piled large rocks and small boulders over the entrance to the cave. Satisfied that hyenas and wolves would have a hard time getting in to the bodies, he picked the cubs up, one under each arm, and set off. He returned at a faster pace and so was only half an hour behind the time he had promised to return.

The others were worried because he was late, and they were surprised on seeing the cubs. Rachel thought they were darling, but she was concerned about feeding them.

"They're past the nursing period," Gribardsun said. "Meat and berries are all they'll need."

He brought out a package which he unfolded on the lee side of the vessel. It was a conical framework about three feet high. He spread a thin sheet of plastic over it, secured its corners, and then sprayed a thick coat of foam over the plastic. The foam dried within ten minutes, and he sprayed another coat and then another. The three coats made a covering four inches thick. He cut a hole at the base for the cubs and used the cutout as a swinging door. The cubs now had a snug warm house.

The bearhouse was a smaller scale model of the dwellings that the humans would erect later on. These were very light and even Rachel could carry one for miles, though the size made them awkward to handle. They could be dragged through the roughest land, however, without damaging them. And axles and wheels, also stored in the vessel, could be attached to them when they were to be moved any distance.

At noon, they were all back at the tribal campsite. This was to be referred to in the official reports, and so unofficially among themselves, as Site A-One or just A-One. Again, they were confronted by a number of warriors. Gribardsun proceeded ahead of his fellows but much more swiftly this time, as if he expected to be received without suspicion. He headed for the tent housing Abinal and entered with a nod to the mother, Amaga. Abinal looked much better. He was frightened on seeing the stranger, but Gribardsun talked in a soothing tone while he examined him. He gave the boy another pill, but the boy refused to swallow it.

Gribardsun, smiling, took out another and swallowed it to show Abinal that it was harmless.

Abinal still turned his face away, and his mother jabbered away at Gribardsun. It seemed she was trying to get him to leave the boy alone.

Gribardsun made signs indicating that Abinal would die if he did not take the pill. He also indicated that the others would die, too, but he was not sure that he was getting his message across.

He left the tent because it was obvious that Abinal was too scared of him to do anything he was going to suggest. Rachel was taking films of a woman skinning a marmot. Drummond was knocking off samples of rocks with a pick while a crowd of children watched him along with several of the men. Robert von Billmann had given an old white-haired woman, who probably wasn't much over fifty-five, some meat, and she was teaching him the language. She was showing him various objects as referents.

Gribardsun decided that their camp should be set up about a quarter-mile down the valley. There was a slight overhang halfway up a steep hill that would give them protection from the weather. They would be close enough to visit the site without wasting much travel time. But they would not be so close that the natives would feel that the aliens were sitting on top of them.

Gribardsun entered the tent again. The boy was being fed by his sister, Laminak, who appeared to be about twelve years old. She looked up startled when Gribardsun came in, but she smiled at him. He smiled back at her and, squatting, felt Abinal's pulse. It was seventy-six, and his skin was warm but moist. Gribardsun stood up and turned away and inserted a panacea into the spout of a bag of water. That the pill would be much diluted did not matter. It was extremely powerful. Moreover, if the others drank from the bag, that was all the better. Gribardsun would have liked to dope all the water bags.

The boy said something, and the girl stood up and faced the Englishman. She spoke to him in a protesting manner. He understood, after a minute, that Abinal had seen him drop something into the water. Gribardsun did not try to deny it. He tried instead to demonstrate, with sign language, that he meant to make Abinal well.

Laminak called out, and Amaga, her mother, entered. There wasn't much room to stand in the tent then. Gribardsun bent over and went out through the narrow, low opening.

"What's going on in there?" Rachel asked.

Gribardsun told her, and she said, "If you get them upset, then we lose our chance to study them at close range."

"And if they all die, then we lose our chance too," he said. "Besides, I can't see letting anyone die if I can prevent it. Even if . . ."

"Even if they're going to die anyway and, in one sense, are already dead?" Rachel said.

He smiled and said, "In that sense, we also are already dead. *And we know it!* But that doesn't stop us from trying to live forever, does it?"

Amaga came out of the tent with the bag of water. She walked to the end of the ledge and poured the water down the hillside. Then, after a quick but triumphant glance at the Englishman, she went back into the tent.

"They won't accept my help," he said. "They're afraid I'll get control of them if they take my medicine, I suppose. And so Abinal may die."

"It's a matter of timing," she said. "If we had only gotten here a week or so sooner, they might have accepted your medicine when Abinal got sick. But . . ."

Gribardsun was not one to dwell long on *what-if's*. If he could not help Abinal now, then he would work to establish confidence in himself through the tribe's elders. He might be able to help Abinal later on. If it was too late then, so be it.

Through sign language, he communicated to the adult males that he had killed two bears—or two large ferocious animals—and that they should follow him to the scene of the kill. They were reluctant. Then, understanding at last that they were afraid to leave the women and children while any of the four stayed behind, he told the others they would have to come with him. Von Billmann protested, but Gribardsun said that their work would go better if he could make these people grateful to him.

Gribardsun also suggested that those women who could be spared should come along with them. After about twenty minutes, they set out with the four aliens in the lead. The natives were still suspicious, but the image of all that meat was too tempting.

Long before he reached the site, Gribardsun knew that someone had been at the bears. Through the slight drizzle, he saw that the stones he had piled up had been torn down and rolled away.

He entered the gap in the rocks slowly, cautiously. There were no humans there, and only parts of the bears remained. The entrails had been left behind, and there was blood on the rocks here and there. However, the robbers had done a relatively neat job.

Gribardsun paid no attention to the furious chatter of the disappointed men and women nor their reproachful expressions. He cast around the area past the rocky floor until he found a footprint in the half-frozen mud. It was filling in swiftly, but there was enough of an outline to show him that a large man with boots or some kind of shoes had slipped off a rock and stepped into the mud.

He went north and within a hundred yards found that a bear's paw had trailed in the mud for several feet. It must have slipped off the shoulders of the man carrying it.

"There must be quite a few in the party," he said to von Billmann. "Those bears together weigh over two thousand pounds, and while they were cut into smaller pieces, no ten men are going to carry the pieces away. I wonder why I wasn't attacked. They must have been watching me while I blocked the gap."

He decided that it was because he was a queerly clothed stranger, and also because they might have been scared by the firing of the rifle.

There was a shout, and they looked up to see a band of six hunters approaching them. These were Glamug, the shaman, Shivkaet, Angrogrim, Gullshab, Dubhab, and the chief, Thammash. They carried pieces of two reindeer wrapped in the skinned-off hides of the animals.

There was a loud and fierce conference with frequent glances and gesticulations at the four strangers.

By now, Gribardsun and von Billmann had learned that the basic word for an adult male bear was *wotaba* and for a female adult bear was *wotaimg*. There were frequent references to both, and Gribardsun could not understand this. Perhaps they knew from the entrails and the single mark of the claw that the animals were bears, but how did they know the sex of each? Then he remembered that some of them had gone into the cave and must have deduced from evidence there that there were beasts of two sexes. He would find out their method of detection when he learned the language.

He interrupted the angry conference by bellowing through the bullhorn at them. Then he made signs

that he would follow the robbers and indicated that
he would like some of them to join him. The robbers
could not be too far ahead, even if they had started
to work immediately after he left the cave. They would
be heavily burdened.

The Silversteins were upset at the turn of events.
Von Billmann appeared ready to do whatever Gribardsun wanted. The Englishman told the Silversteins to
return to the campsite with the natives. He and the
German, and some of the men, if they would agree,
would track the robbers.

"But we can't get involved in the quarrels of these
people!" Drummond said. "We don't want to get into
the position of having to take sides! Maybe even having to kill their enemies!"

"We'll have to play favorites," Gribardsun said.
"There's no way of getting away from it. Moreover,
the more deeply these people are in our debt, the
sooner they'll open up for us. We can't stay neutral."

"You have no right to shoot those men!" Drummond Silverstein said.

"Who said I would shoot them?" Gribardsun said,
staring hard at Silverstein. "Why don't you ask me what
I intend to do instead of making your assumptions?"

"I'm sorry," Silverstein said. "Perhaps I'm wrong.
But I don't see how you can attempt to take all that
meat away from these savages without having to fight
them."

"I have to re-establish our prestige," the Englishman
said. "Otherwise we'll never be able to know these
people inside and out. I've said that twice. Once should
be enough."

He turned away. "Come on, Robert."

Four of the tribesmen joined them, among them
Thammash and the giant Angrogrim. They set out
northward with the Englishman in the lead. He trotted

along, looking to both sides for signs. After a mile he saw a track, and a little farther on where a man had spit. Then they entered a morass which held many prints. Gribardsun thought that the party was composed of fourteen men.

They crossed a plain while going toward some hills about a hundred feet high on the horizon. In the distance, to both left and right, were herds of grey-brown mammoths and brownish reindeer. A pack of a dozen hyenas skulked along behind the reindeer. A brown-gray fox sped across the plain after a hare and presently caught it. And then Gribardsun saw their quarry far across the plain. They were all, except for six rear-guard men, half covered with parts of the bears.

Gribardsun slowed his pace to allow von Billmann to draw even with him. Von Billmann was panting, though he had gone through the rigorous yearlong physical training prior to the launching. The hunters trotted along, their breaths slightly steaming as the late afternoon turned even colder, the slush splashing over their bare legs. They did not seem in the least hard pressed.

"The two tribes would have come into contact sooner or later anyway," Gribardsun said. "One of them probably has only recently moved into this territory. I intend to scare this one away so our subject-study will be left alone."

"But we want to study their war patterns, too," von Billmann said.

"That can come later."

As he ran he was taking films of the men ahead, the area around, and of the men trotting along behind. He ran backward as swiftly as he ran forward while he filmed those behind.

By the time they got across the plain, they had lost their quarry, vanished up a pass between two low hills. Here were dead winter grasses with lichen on the rocks and dwarf birches and pines and some beds of saxifrage. A black and white badger waddled away from them as they ran into the pass.

Gribardsun supposed that the men they were following had seen them, so he halted his party after it had gone a few yards into the pass. Ahead, the hills grew taller and started to move closer. A brook about five feet wide followed the middle of the pass downward towards the plain, where it suddenly turned and followed the edge of the hills toward the west.

Gribardsun in the lead, his express rifle ready, the party moved slowly up the pass. He expected an ambush, but they got through the pass without incident. They came out onto a small valley which had been formed by a small river. Across the river, up near the top of the hill opposite, was an overhang. This was walled on two sides with piles of stones, and in between were skin tents, tiny at this distance, and a blue haze of smoke under the projecting rock. The robbers were fording the river, and the rearguards were waving at those under the overhang. And, no doubt, they were shouting an alarm.

By the time the invaders reached the bottom of the valley, they could hear the shrilling of bone whistles and flutes and the beat of skin-and-wood drums.

The four tribesmen were looking at each other out of the corners of their eyes and muttering. They were glad to stop at the river when Gribardsun paused to take stock.

"It's not just a matter of a territorial imperative," von Billmann said. "We're heavily outnumbered. I'm surprised they've gone this far with us."

"They know from my signs that I have killed two bears so they must have some faith in my skill, even if they don't know how it was done," Gribardsun said. "But I wouldn't be surprised if they ran anyway."

The ledge under the overhang was alive with men brandishing weapons. Other men, hunters returning, were hastening up the hill to join the defense. The defense, Gribardsun thought, which may soon become an offense. There are only six of us.

However, the robbers must believe that one of the invaders had killed two bears with a loud noise. And that meant that the noisemaker was a powerful magician. He would have control over great and mysterious forces. And it was their fear of these forces that Gribardsun depended upon in his plan.

The four natives, however, did not cross the ford. They stood on the bank and gazed apprehensively at the display of spears and clubs on the ledge. Gribardsun turned when he was across the river, shouted at them and made encouraging motions. But they would not follow.

The Englishman took the small Very pistol from his sack, loaded it, and fired it into the air. The explosions and colors silenced the noisy mob on the ledge. Before the flare had parachuted to the ground, the four natives were across the river and standing by Gribardsun's side. They looked pale and grim, but they had evidently decided that it would not be good to offend this witch doctor.

The six advanced slowly up the hillside. Halfway up, they halted. The defenders were behind a row of large boulders along the rim of the ledge, undoubtedly only waiting to shove them over once the intruders were closer.

Gribardsun emptied his express rifle and reloaded with five high-explosive bullets. He aimed at the center boulder on the edge and fired the bullets, one after the other.

The boulder was a heap of fragments.

The warriors had disappeared.

Gribardsun reloaded with explosive bullets and continued climbing. Before reaching the ledge, however, he stopped and shot three times into the overhang just underneath its edge. Several large pieces of rock fell off. Screams followed the explosions, and warriors, women, and children deserted the site. They fled in two streams down the sides of the ledge and on down the hillside, falling, leaping up again, yelling, shrilling mindlessly.

"I hope they don't hurt themselves," Gribardsun said.

Their four natives were whooping with joy and slapping each other on the back or the thighs. Then Angrogrim started toward the refugees on their right. He held his spear high, shaking it, and screaming threats at them.

Gribardsun called after him, but the giant continued to run toward the refugees. The Englishman fired into the air, and Angrogrim turned to see what he was doing. Gribardsun gestured fiercely at him to come back. Scowling, the giant obeyed. Gribardsun shook his finger at him and scolded him as if he were a child. Angrogrim looked down at him as if he thought he was very odd. But he did not protest, and when he saw the others continue their climb, he followed them.

At the top, they looked around the deserted site. Von Billmann used his movie camera. Gribardsun looked cautiously through the tents and found an old man and woman cowering in one and a sick five-year-old child in the other. He got the child to swallow a panacea and then ran the diagnoser over his body and took a sample of blood.

The old couple were almost toothless, and the woman was blind. Both shook so violently that they could not answer when Thammash spoke to them. Finally, the woman replied, and Thammash raised his eyebrows, shrugged his shoulders, and turned his palms upward. It was evident that he did not understand the woman's language.

Von Billmann made signs that Thammash should continue to elicit speech from the couple. But Thammash was more interested in loot. He and the others were busy prowling around, inspecting and appropriating flint and bone spearheads, atlatls, bone fishhooks, and needles and bone and ivory figurines.

Gribardsun watched them carefully, and when he saw Gullshab enter the tent of the sick child, he went after him. He was just in time to stop him from plunging his spear into the boy's solar plexus. Gullshab was somewhat resentful, but he understood that the child was not to be harmed, and he passed the message along to the others.

However, Angrogrim did not think that the restriction applied to the old couple. He picked up a club and started toward the oldsters' tent but stopped when Gribardsun shouted at him. He threw the club down angrily and walked off.

Gribardsun made signs that each should pick up a piece of bear and start back. It would be dusk within half an hour. It was evident that they would have to leave at least half of the bear meat behind, so several of the men started to foul it. Gribardsun ordered them to stop, and when they pretended they did not understand him, he made threatening signs. Reluctantly, they turned away and hoisted the meat they had chosen onto their shoulders.

"I just wanted to scare the strangers away so we could recover some of the meat and thus impress both parties," Gribardsun said. "I see no reason why we can't contact these people later and perhaps conduct studies of them, too."

Gribardsun hoisted a hind leg of cave bear upon his shoulder and led his band back down the hill. The refugees had halted their mad flight and the two groups were now standing near the bottom of the hill and watching the strangers. The six men proceeded slowly and carefully under their burdens, unhindered by the two groups. After they had crossed the river, they did hear threatening shouts but these were mere bravado. None of the shouters ran after them to throw spears.

Darkness fell swiftly. The wind died down, but the air got even colder. A lion roared about half a mile to the west. A mammoth trumpeted shrilly. Something snorted deeply behind a hillock.

The four natives talked to each other in low but happy voices and occasionally said something to Gribardsun or von Billmann. They did not expect to be understood, but they just wanted the two to know that they were not being excluded from the geniality.

Gribardsun turned on his flashlight, causing the men to moan with awe. They dropped behind for a while as if they were afraid of the light. But when a lion coughed about a hundred yards in their rear, they crowded upon the Englishman's heels.

Their entrance to the campsite was a victorious one. The Silversteins turned their flashlights on them as they came up the hillside, and then torches flared as the people streamed down to shout with joy at sight of the meat. Once on the ledge under the overhang, the four men recounted their adventures. The others looked with awe at Gribardsun. Gribardsun took advantage of his increased prestige to enter the tent where Abinal lay and give him another panacea. Abinal was sicker, and Gribardsun was not sure that

the pill would do him much good. In fact, he would
not have been surprised if the boy were dead by
morning. He hoped not. Aside from his human concern, he didn't want to be blamed for the boy's death.
He did not like the looks which Glamug, the shaman,
gave him when he came out of the tent. If the boy
lived, Glamug would try to take the credit. If the
boy died, Glamug would put the responsibility on the
stranger.

The shaman had put on a headband of grouse
feathers and, with a bag full of medicine-magic objects and a reindeer's bladder filled with pebbles tied
to the end of a stick, was dancing slowly around the
tent. He chanted in a shrill voice while he danced.
Amaga, the mother, stood by the flap of the tent with
a pine torch and waved it around in circles. The father,
Dubhab, had painted his forehead with a mixture of
wood ash and some dark clay, but he took no part in
the ceremony. He sat by a hearth and ate roast bear
and seemed to be cracking jokes with some of his
hearthmates.

After a while Glamug, tired by the day's hunting
and the trek after the stolen meat, flopped down
by the hearth. Rachel quit taking films of the ceremony. Drummond squatted by a hearth and chewed on
a piece of bear meat while his black eyes moved from
side to side. He looked tired and had already mentioned that he would like to go home. Robert von
Billmann was recording a speech by Dubhab, who
seemed to be telling of the raid.

The villagers (Gribardsun was thinking of the place
as a village) were occupied in having a good time,
though some were busy with chores that could not be
put off. Some young mothers were suckling their babies,
which were wrapped up in furs. A middle-aged woman
had stuffed herself with meat and now was chewing on

a piece of skin to make it soft. An hour and a half passed, and most had crawled into their tents and tied down the flaps to keep out the wind. The fires in the hearths were covered with ashes; the coals would be revivified in the morning.

Dubhab and Amaga and the girl, Laminak, had retired into the tent with the sick boy. Glamug danced again around the tent, chanting in a low voice, shaking his rattle, and occasionally making a sign at the four major points of the compass. He folded his thumb and two middle fingers together and extended his little finger and index finger. All four of the scientists noted the sign; it was indeed an ancient one.

Glamug soon tired again. But he did not enter his tent, even though his wife had stuck her head out from time to time and looked at him as she wished he would come home. Glamug got a huge bison fur and wrapped himself in it while he sat in front of the sick boy's tent. His head was hidden in a great fold of the fur, but one hand was out in the cold, holding the reindeer bladder. Evidently he was on duty all night, guarding against the spirit of sickness and death.

The scientists decided to call it a day. They started out on the cold and weary walk to the vessel. The village was quiet; there were no guards; even Glamug was snoring in the depths of his robe.

The next morning they ate a good breakfast and rehashed the previous day's events. Rachel and Gribardsun fed the bear cubs and played with them a little. Rachel seemed happier than the day before. Gribardsun wondered if it was because she was with him. She smiled much at him, laughed at almost everything he said, and reached out and put her hand on his arm or shoulder and once moved her fingertip along his jaw. He was aware that yesterday's events had raised him even further in her esteem. Whatever was driving the Silversteins apart was carrying her toward him. He did not believe that he was the original force that had split them. But he might get blamed before they settled their troubles.

He decided that he would have to talk seriously to her, perhaps to both of them, apart or together, and straighten them out. But he did not think that now was the time for it. He would put it off for a while. If he did so, then her interest in him might die away, or she might find means to sublimate it, or she and her husband might come to terms with their differences. He believed much in allowing time to effect cures.

The next job was to move the building materials to the site chosen for their camp. Carrying large packs, they hiked to the ledge, where it took them only an hour to erect two beehive-shaped buildings. Since these were so light that a strong wind could carry them away, they were enclosed around the bases with piles of stones. And some small boulders were placed on the floor inside to secure them even further. The Silversteins moved into one building; the Englishman and German into the other.

At noon they returned to the vessel and packed more materials. They carried these to the "village," where the women and children and a few men crowded around them in wonder. The people were amazed at the spraying and hardening of the foam. Only after some talk among themselves did they get courage enough to approach and touch the plastic. They watched as the four piled stones around these and placed some heavy ones inside. Gribardsun cut out the door and replaced it with hinges and a lock. This dome was to hold artifacts and records and specimens and to serve as a temporary home and workshop. Gribardsun walked around it twelve times chanting

Carroll's *The Hunting of the Snark* and making meaningless gestures. He hoped by doing this to convince the villagers that magic was being invoked to protect the dome.

After that, he went in Abinal's tent and found the boy sitting up and eating meat from a bone. The boy, who had been laughing with his sister, fell silent as Gribardsun entered. But Laminak spoke a few words to him, and he relaxed somewhat. Gribardsun examined him, noticing that the boy shrank from the touch of his fingers. But his sister jollied him, and she even spoke to Gribardsun, though she knew he could not understand her.

When the Englishman and the girl left the tent, he pointed at various people or objects and asked Laminak their names. She caught on and entered the game with enthusiasm. She was a pretty girl in spite of the dirt and the cumbersome fur she wore. Her hair was waist-length, wavy, and would, if washed, have been a rich chestnut color. Her face was broad but her nose was medium in size and well shaped. Her lips were full and grease-smeared, like those of her fellows, to avoid chapping. Her breasts were just beginning to swell. She had large dark eyes that looked merry most of the time. And she seemed to lack the fear for him that the others had.

He liked her very much, and this liking reinforced her attitude to him. She was intelligent; she was soon putting the names of objects into short sentences for his benefit. Or, rather, as he discovered, incorporating them into words, since the language of the *Wota'shaimg* lacked sentences in the English meaning of the word. A Wota'shaimg "sentence" was a "word," a string of syllables or single phones attached to each other in a certain sequence with the object-term as the nucleus.

Later, Gribardsun and von Billmann were to agree

that the structure of the speech of the Bear Folk had striking parallels to the structure of both Eskimo and Shawnee. The sounds were different, of course, and Wota'shaimg had no relation to either of those two languages.

Von Billmann, who was fluent in both Basque and Georgian, could determine no relationship between Wota'shaimg and either of those languages. He admitted that his studies of a possible relationship were superficial and that a deep study by many scholars might reveal a kinship. But he doubted it.

Von Billmann's field was Indo-Hittite with Celtic as his specialization. But he had been highly trained in other fields, including American Indian languages. No one else was as competent as he to study the middle Magdalenian tongues.

Chapter 2

The days and nights went by swiftly. The sun became hotter, and the earth bloomed. The women left the area to dig for roots and collect medicinal plants and edible berries. They also tanned the skins their men brought in, cut them into desired shapes, and sewed them with ivory or bone needles and thin gut-thread. They spent endless hours chewing hides to make them soft. They smoked meat in little huts on racks. They worked from dawn to far past dusk.

A baby was born to Gragmirri, a young woman. Gribardsun wanted to assist, or at least to make sure that the delivery was sanitary. But the birth took place in a specially erected tent to which no men, not even Glamug, the shaman, were admitted. And both the baby boy and the mother did well. Gragmirri was up and working the second day, and the men were handling the baby and exclaiming over its fine physique. Glamug sprinkled some milk on its head, and the bear cub licked the milk off while the baby cried and Glamug loudly chanted. By then the four were versed enough in the language to know that the baby, Shamkunnap, had been initiated into the tribe. He was now a member of the family of the Great Bear, and if

46

he died he would go to a place where the Great Bear, some sort of ancestral spirit, would provide him with all the comforts of life.

The four scientists worked almost as hard as the Bear People. They made records and films and collected specimens. Drummond and Rachel took short field trips. He studied the geology of the area, she collected specimens of plant and animal life and of soil and made many photographs.

The days were getting warm enough so that they need wear only shorts and shoes. One day, Gribardsun started to wear native garb entirely. At this season, that consisted of a skin loincloth and a broad leather belt. He even went barefooted, revealing to his fellow scientists feet with thick calluses on the soles.

"If you had a beard, you could pass for a Wota'-shaimg," Rachel said. She looked admiringly at his powerfully muscled yet beautifully proportioned body.

"You could play Tarzan in the trivis," she said.

Drummond did not look happy. He said, "Where in hell did you get those calluses?"

"I never wore shoes when I lived in Africa," the Englishman said. "You know that I spent many years on the Inner Kenyan Sanctuary. The natives there were barefoot; so I was barefoot too."

Gribardsun's black hair was shoulder-length after the fashion that had come in two years before, and he wore bangs across his forehead. He looked even more savage than the savages, since his skin was a uniform bronze but theirs was pale except on the face and the arms. During the past few days he had taken to throwing a spear with an atlatl at a target of wood and grass that he had built. Though he practiced only half an hour a day, he was becoming very accurate. And he could already throw a spear about twenty yards beyond the best cast of Angrogrim, the champion of the Wota'shaimg.

This accomplishment did not lessen his attractions for Rachel.

"I always thought that the Cro-Magnons, having much sturdier bones for muscle attachments, would be stronger than modern men," she said.

"These aren't the very early Cro-Magnons," von Billmann said. "But even so, they are large, and their constant use of their muscles in hunting and labor should make them very strong. In fact, they are stronger than Drummond or me. Even their smallest, Dubhab, is stronger. But the *duke* seems to be an exception. Indeed, if I thought such a thing possible, I'd say he is an atavism, a throwback. But he just happens to be exceptionally powerful."

Von Billmann sometimes referred to the Englishman as *the duke,* or His Grace. The reference was not altogether sarcastic. Von Billmann had a high regard for Gribardsun which was not, however, unmixed with envy.

The four were by the riverbank at the bottom of the valley below the village site. The German was sitting in a folding chair and transcribing notes from the playback of his recorder. Drummond was breaking open some geodes with his hammer. Rachel had been collecting pollen samples, but she had stopped to watch the spear-atlatl practice.

"John said he meant to take part in the first big hunt," she said. "He wants to carry only native weapons."

"Admirable, this desire to get into the subjects' skin," Drummond said, looking up from an egg-shaped rock. "But I think he's carrying it too far. What if he gets killed? What benefit will that be to science?"

"I would think you'd like—" Rachel said and then closed her mouth.

"Like him to be killed?" Drummond said in a low but fierce voice. "Do you really believe I'm jealous of him? Should I be? Have you given me any reason?"

"Don't be a fool!" Rachel said. Her face was red. She turned and walked away a few feet but stopped by von Billmann's chair.

"I don't know what's the matter with him!" she said, half to herself, half to von Billmann. "He was acting a little peculiar a few weeks before we launched. But since then he's gotten terrible. Do you think that there's something about this world, or about being cut off from his own time, that . . . ?"

"Has Drummond checked the excess or lack of certain ions in the atmosphere?"

"He has, but I don't remember the results," she said. "It should have been the first thing I thought of. But I haven't noticed any change in my behavior. Or yours. Or John's."

"I don't know about John," von Billmann said. "I've always detected a certain *je-ne-sais-quoi* about John, a certain repressed—uh—what the nineteenth-century writers called *animal magnetism*. Do you know what I mean?"

"Yes," she said, looking at Gribardsun as he straightened up after a throw. The hand that held the long notched atlatl turned, and the muscles leaped out along his arm.

"There's something strange about him," von Billmann said. "I've known him, off and on, for twenty years. There's something of the wild beast about him. I don't mean that he's bestial, or degraded. He's one of nature's gentlemen, to use another archaic phrase. But there's definitely something scary deep down under that handsome hide."

"The spear went dead center in the bull's eye," she said. "I don't see how anybody using that stick can get any accuracy."

That evening the four sat around a hearth with Dubhab's family and watched pieces of deer sizzle on the ends of sticks they held. They were visiting Dubhab today; tomorrow, Wazwim's family would be their hosts. To avoid any show of favoritism, the four visited each family by turn. This rotation also enabled them to become more familiar with each family. And, since each had his own pet interests, the visitors could get a broader view of Magdalenian society. Dubhab, for instance, a short very hairy man with bright blue eyes and thin lips, was a born trader. Rather, he was a born confidence man, since he was always trying to get something for nothing or, at least, for very little.

Dubhab also liked to listen to himself talk and so he would launch into a lecture on almost any subject if he thought he had an audience. The four picked up much information—and a lot of superstitions and misinformation—about many things. But even the folk tales and the wrong data were information. They were part of the picture of what the Wota'shaimg believed.

Amaga was about Dubhab's age, somewhere between thirty-two and thirty-eight. She lacked five front teeth and a number of back teeth. Smallpox had scarred her face, as it had of half the tribe. Her naked breasts were huge and pendulous, though she informed them that they had been high and firm when she was a young woman. She had married Dubhab because he seemed to be on his way to the chieftainship. And he had been a very good provider. But later, he talked more than he acted, and he was always trying to get the better of others in a bargain. So he had become just another mediocre hunter, and he talked more than any woman, and she had, in effect, thrown herself away on him.

She did not say all this in front of Dubhab, of course, because he would have beaten her if she had demeaned his manhood in public. But, inside the walls of her tent, Amaga told him what she told the strangers.

Abinal, the son, was a "normal" boy. He wanted to be a mighty hunter, and perhaps a chief, and he played at these fantasies when he wasn't working. His work consisted of learning to hunt, which was no work at all for him, and how to pick berries and other plants in the summer. He shuttled back and forth between learning a man's work and a woman's work. When he came of age—at twelve or thereabouts—he would go through the rites of passage and no longer help the women.

Laminak's rites would be conducted by the women in the summer in some place hidden from men's eyes. In the meantime, she was becoming a woman without getting official approval. She worshipped John Gribardsun and frequently made a nuisance of herself by hanging around when he wanted private talks with others. But he did not get angry.

Tonight, Dubhab was trying to get Gribardsun to promise him the horn of a rhinoceros or the tusks of a mammoth. Tomorrow, the Wota'shaimg were going on a big hunt, and the four strangers—the *Sha'shinq*—were going along. Dubhab was certain that Gribardsun would kill some of the big game with his loud noise stick, and he wanted a gift. The horn of a rhinoceros, set before the tent of a warrior, ensured that that man would have strength and courage and prosperity. The tusk of a mammoth was also valuable for several reasons.

John Gribardsun politely refused several times, saying that whoever deserved the horns or tusks, according to the customs of the Wota'shaimg, would get them. Dubhab argued that it was a certainty that Gribardsun would kill many with the stick. Why couldn't he see his way clear to giving Dubhab at least one?

Finally Gribardsun, irked, said that he did not want to hear any more about it. For one thing, he did not plan to use his thunder stick. Von Billman would be carrying it, but he would use it only if he had to. He, Gribardsun, would be with the hunters and using the same weapons they used.

Dubhab swallowed his disappointment and managed to smile at the Englishman. Gribardsun—or Koorik, as he was called, meaning Thunder Death—would be a mighty hunter even with ordinary weapons. He would surely slay a dozen great beasts with his spear alone. Why couldn't he . . . ?

Gribardsun disliked cutting the man off because of his fondness for Laminak. But he stood up, bade them good night, and walked off. The others were caught by surprise, but they followed him. He went to the fire around which sat Thummash, the chief, Wazwim, the singer, Glamug, the shaman, and Angrogrim, the strong man. It was the custom that everyone say good night to the chief before retiring, and Gribardsun tried to live within the customs as well as he could.

The men had been squatting by the big hearths. Over this pile of stones the head men of the Wota'-shaimg gathered each evening. As the four approached the hearth, the head men stood up. Glamug got up last, not because of any reluctance to honor them, but because of his rheumatism. Though he might have resented the presence of mightier magicians, he did not seem to do so. He had already hinted that if they had anything to alleviate rheumatism, he would be most grateful. His dancing was becoming steadily more painful. Gribardsun had said that he would see what he could do. He was studying his medical books in the late evenings, seeking a cure for Glamug's ailment. Rheumatism was unknown in modern days though not when he was a young man. But he had paid it no attention then, and when he became an M.D. fairly late in life, he had never had reason to learn much about it.

The party had been inoculated against every disease supposed to be rampant in the Pleistocene, but since they were genetically invulnerable to rheumatism, they had taken no shots nor brought along any books about the disease. This was one of the curious omissions that the expedition ran across every now and then. It was well known, from a study of the bones of middle Magdalenian man, that rheumatism and kindred arthritic diseases were common. But, somehow, these had been overlooked.

Actually, the planners could not be blamed. It was not part of the expedition's purpose to cure the people they found. Their primary mission was to study. Any good they could scatter along the way would be up to their individual decisions.

The head men said good night in turn, the chief speaking first. The four set off through the darkness, their lights probing ahead. Near their camp, they heard squeals and then a chilling laugh. They hurried and were in time to see several huge hyenas slink off. They had been trying to get into the dome in which the two pet bears were kept.

When the expedition had first come, the hyenas had seemed fairly common. But when warmer weather came, the Wota'shaimg had hunted down all the large predators in the neighborhood, including the hyenas. These big brutes were dangerous, since they often hunted in packs, were not at all cowardly, and had jaws stronger than a cave lion's. But many of them died, and in a short time they ventured out only at night in this area. But the few left did venture quite close to the two human habitations.

Gribardsun checked to make sure that the bears were unharmed and that their food and water supply was full. Then he went into his own dome with von Billmann after saying good night to the Silversteins. He fell asleep quickly but was awakened at three o'clock by his alarm. He shook the German awake, and they ate breakfast. Von Billmann dressed in hiking clothes with boots, but Gribardsun put on the skin loincloth and threw a fur cloak over his shoulders. They went outside, where the Silversteins were just leaving their dome. They set out for the overhang, drinking coffee from their thermos and saying little.

At the village, they found a bonfire going, before which the hunters, adults and juveniles sat. The women and children sat about twenty yards away and made no noise during the ceremony that followed.

The strangers, except for Rachel, sat down at the right end of the hunters. Though she was not forbidden to take part in the hunt, she was not allowed to participate in the ceremony. She sat with the women.

As the dawn turned the world blue and green, Glamug came out from his tent. He was naked except for a reindeer loin covering, a rhinoceros skull over his head, and a cloak of bear fur. His body was painted with ocher, green, brown, black, and yellow symbols. One of these was a swastika with its arms to the right, the good-luck gammadion. This was the first time any of the four had seen this, though there were a variety of other types of crosses painted on the skins of the tents.

Rachel filmed Glamug; Gribardsun made a mental note to comment in the vessel's log on the earliest recorded appearance of the ancient and once honorable symbol.

Glamug held in one hand a rhinoceros tail and in the other two small painted figurines of a rhinoceros and a mammoth. These were made of ground bone dust mixed with ocher and bear fat and baked in a small stone oven.

Glamug danced before the hunters, shaking the rhino tail and occasionally flicking the hunters in the face with its tip. He chanted a song which the Silversteins understood not at all and which the other two comprehended only partially. After a while the two men perceived that the chant was a linguistic fossil, preserved from an earlier stage of the language. It was as if a modern Englishman were to sing a song in Middle English to an audience which did not know what half of the words meant. Gribardson looked at von Billmann, who was grinning with delight at this treasure trove of speech.

At the end of the ceremony, Glamug cast each of the figurines into the flame after reciting a short but savage prayer over each figure. As the rhino and mammoth figurines were thrown into the fire, the hunters bellowed or made a trumpeting sound.

Immediately thereafter, Glamug ran to the temporary tents at one corner of the ledge and got his weapons. All of the hunters had slept there last night, jammed against each other, keeping each other warm with their body heat. The night before a hunt for any of the large and dangerous beasts, the hunters slept away from all women. Nor were they to be touched by the women until they returned from the hunt and went through a ceremony to propitiate the ghosts of the slain beasts. The women went through a separate, cleansing ceremony before they received their mates in their tents.

The man who led the hunters to the plains was not the chief nor the shaman nor the greatest hunter, Shivkaet. He was a youth, Thrimk, who had gone through the rites of passage only two years before.

Last night he had dreamed that he had encountered a family of rhinos in a narrow valley debouching onto the plain. And in the dream he had slain the male. For this reason he was given the lead, and the hunters sang about his prowess-to-be as they marched along.

When they reached the edge of the plain, they fell silent. They formed into three crescents with the greatest hunters in the first. Gribardsun was put on the right-hand tip of the first crescent. Von Billmann stayed to one side of the group, shooting film. He carried the express rifle. Drummond Silverstein was with the German, though he had originally said that he had too much work to do to accompany them. But he had changed his mind.

Fleetingly, Gribardsun wondered if Silverstein was hoping that his rival (as he undoubtedly thought of him) would get killed. He was the only one who had not protested when Gribardsun said he was going to hunt with only native arms.

Silverstein, however, could not win. If Gribardsun was killed or hurt, then Silverstein's guilt would punish him. If Gribardsun performed well, then Rachel would regard him even more highly, and Silverstein would dislike him even more.

The youth, Thrimk, went straight to the pass giving onto the narrow valley he had seen in his dream. Of course, he must have seen it in reality more than once. Though the valley was six miles away from the village, it was within the territory ranged by the Wota'shaimg. The tribesmen had not come here recently, however, for fear of encountering the other people who had moved in. The Wota'shaimg called these the *Wotagrub*, the Bear Robbers.

The contacts of the two people had been few and brief after the invasion of the Wotagrub's village. The Wotagrub fled whenever they met Wota'shaimg, even though the latter were outnumbered. Once, however, a lone youth—Thrimk, in fact—had almost been hit by a heavy boomerang. The weapon had come sailing from a pile of boulders on the side of a hill. Thrimk had foolishly tried to locate his assailant, but the man was gone.

The head men had urged Gribardsun to clean out the Wotagrum, saying that there was not enough game in the area to support their own people for long, let alone an additional tribe. Moreover, the Wotagrub had not been punished enough for their theft.

Gribardsun had refused. He had nothing against the so-called Wotagrub, who had done only what their enemies would have done in their place. Moreover, though he did not tell the Wota'shaimg so, he intended to study the Wotagrub. And he certainly could not get friendly with them if he decimated them.

The hunters stopped when Thammash raised his hand with a spear held straight up in it. He nodded at Thrimk, who had also stopped. The youth shook his spear at them, smiled, and trotted off into the pass. He was a tall fellow with light brown hair and a scraggly beard. He had not yet attained his full growth. He was noted for his swift running and his high spirits, alternating with fits of deep depression. His father was Kaemgrom, the best worker in stone and wood weapons in the tribe. But Thrimk and his father quarreled often.

The nucleus of the best hunters, with Kaemgrom, who was supposed to stay close to his son, and Gribardsun, trotted after Thrimk a minute later. Von Billman climbed the side of the hill on one side of the gap, and Silverstein climbed the other side to take pictures.

A narrow stream wandered out of the mouth of the valley. Along its sides were unusually heavy growths of vegetation, though none were over six feet high.

Gribardsun saw the vegetation moving. Occasionally Thrimk's head would appear. Then he saw the brown tip of a horn plowing through the little trees. He repressed a shout.

A moment later he heard the sudden thudding of heavy feet and the thrashing of little trees bending and breaking under the onslaught of a huge body.

Thrimk should have gone in far more cautiously, and he should have tried to lure the behemoths out into the open. But he must have been overconfident because of his dream. And he also probably wanted to impress the tribesmen with his bravery.

Whatever his reasons, he had made a fatal mistake.

Thrimk yelled, there was a very loud thud, and the youth's body went sailing through the air while a tall horn followed it and then the shorter horn appeared and then the head of the rhinoceros as the beast completed the upward toss.

Both beast and man disappeared, but the vegetation waved and shook as the beast turned and charged again.

The hunters were setting up loud cries by now. They ran up to the edge of the vegetation and poked their spears into it and shouted. Gribardsun looked up at von Billmann. Gribardsun was not wearing the tiny communication set today. Now he regretted not having permitted himself any product of civilization.

The German, however, saw him and waved at him. Then he gestured into the valley and held up seven fingers. Seven rhinos.

Presently the vegetation thrashed and bent and cracked again, and a great woolly rhinoceros burst out. He was larger than any the group had yet seen, and his hide was covered with brownish tightly coiled hair like rather sparse sheep's wool.

He stopped after he broke the greenery, snuffed, and then trotted back and forth, his head lifted high.

A female and her baby broke out of the woods and then another male and female and a baby and a half-grown female.

The first beast had blood upon his horn and on his hoofs.

Kaemgron yelled and ran forward and then cast his spear. It struck the huge male on the shoulder, and the tip of reindeer antler penetrated about two inches. The atlatl had given the spear considerable force.

At that the rhino, which had not been able to make up its mind which way to charge, or, indeed, to charge at all, started out for Kaemgron. The earth shook as its heavy legs pounded, and its head was slung low.

Kaemgron turned and ran.

Angrogrim threw his spear, and the missile penetrated perhaps three inches into the right rear flank just forward of the upper part of the leg. But the rhino did not even seem aware of the wound.

Other spears missed or, striking, bounced off harmlessly.

The men scattered.

The rhino did not allow itself to be distracted by all the yelling and running figures. It headed straight for Kaemgron and was going to catch up with him within the next twenty or so yards.

The second male also charged.

Gribardsun ran in with a spear he had snatched from a man in flight, and rammed it into the eye of the beast as it passed him by at three feet.

The spear was torn out of his grasp, and he was whirled around violently and thrown to the ground.

Von Billmann's express rifle boomed, and the second rhino stumbled, recovered, and charged again, though not as vigorously. Its goal was Gribardsun, who was just getting to his feet.

The express boomed twice, and the rhino collapsed, its legs folding under it. Blood ran out of three wounds on its left side and out of its mouth.

The first behemoth was also dead. Gribardsun's spear had driven into its brain.

The remaining beasts had turned uncertainly and moved back into the brake. Von Billmann signaled that they were now moving rapidly up the valley. Gribardsun picked up one of the spears that had ricocheted off the beast and went into the brake. It did not take long to find what remained of the unfortunate Thrimk.

Kaemgron pushed past Gribardsun and then wailed loudly. He went around the corpse three times widdershins, dragging his speartip in the earth, and then he returned to the body of the rhino that had killed Thrimk. There he beat the animal over the head with the butt of his spear, wailing and weeping all the time. Then he walked three times counterwiddershins around the beast and cut off its tail with his flint knife. He gave the tail to Gribardsun, who stuck it in his belt. Gribardsun recovered his spear, noting that the reindeer antler tip was loose.

Kaemgron returned to his son's body to mourn. Those who followed him also began wailing. But those who stayed to cut up the two carcasses were jubilant. They laughed and smeared blood over their foreheads and lips and dipped their index fingers in the blood and spotted Gribardsun's forehead with the blood. After von Billmann came down off the hillside, he was daubed with blood, too.

"That was very good shooting, Robert," Gribardsun said.

"I've practiced enough in the preserve," von Billmann said. "But you, you were magnificent! Right through the eye, and you had to crouch and drive it upward, the rhino's head was so low! If it had turned on you . . ."

"But it didn't," the Englishman said. "He had his heart set on Kaemgron. Though it is true that the beasts are very unpredictable and he might have turned."

He did not seem to want to talk about his feat. But he looked as if he were bursting with happiness.

Drummond joined them. He said, "I got some fine shots, but the people back home aren't going to believe them."

Thammash approached Gribardsun. "We have plenty of meat for a week or so," he said. "And the mourning for Thrimk must start soon. But the day is far from being over, and it would be well if we pushed on and killed more. What do you think?"

Though he had been treated with great politeness and respect from the beginning, Gribardsun had not before been asked to decide any course of action. Apparently his spectacular feat had made him the equal, or perhaps even the superior, of the chief. He was now one of them—in some respects anyway.

Von Billmann had been daubed with the rhino blood, and he was treated with great respect too. But the tribesmen seemed to believe that he was secondary to the Englishman. Perhaps they thought this because Gribardsun, being the first one to use the rifle, was considered to be the owner. And he had loaned his thunder stick while he killed the rhino with unmagical weapons to show that he could use them as no one else could.

Gribardsun considered and then said, "We should push on, I believe. Why waste the day?"

The body of Thimk was wrapped in a great bearskin

and six men were delegated to watch the body and to cut up the two behemoths. Leaving these behind weakened the party, but the hyenas, wolves, lions and bears had to be kept away.

The party set out again toward the edge of the plain where a herd of mammoths was eating. The great beasts did not pay them any attention until the hunters were within fifty yards. They were downwind, and the mammoths, like the elephants of Gribardsun's time, were weak-eyed. But when they detected the mass of humans, they began moving away. Several big bulls, however, threatened them with short charges and much trumpeting and tearing up of small trees.

The very long and fantastically curved tusks, the huge hump of fat on top of the head, the long reddish-brown hairs, and the sheer size of the beasts was very impressive.

The men spread out in a deep crescent formation. While the center held the attention of the bulls, the horns advanced very slowly.

One of the bulls broke and ran toward the herd.

The other two kept up their bluffing charges until the center had gotten within fifty feet and the horns of the crescent were past them.

Then the biggest bull charged.

The plan was for the center to turn and flee, drawing the beast after it. The horns would close in and try to hamstring or spear the beast.

The center was not imitating panic. Its members were scared, and rightly so. The beast was over eleven feet high at the shoulder, weighed possibly four tons, and was running faster than any man.

Only Gribardsun did not run. He waited with his spear butt resting against the notch of the atlatl. When the beast was a shrilling gray and reddish-brown wall with great curving ivory tusks and uplifted trunk and big outspread ears and little red eyes, only thirty feet away, he sped to one side.

The mammoth started to turn toward him, but it wasn't fast enough. Gribardsun cast the spear from the atlatl, and half its length disappeared into the beast's left front leg.

The animal went down with a crash that must have broken some of its bones.

Trumpeting agonizedly, it struggled to get back onto its feet.

The hunters ran in and lunged, driving their flint or reindeer antler-tipped spearheads into the stomach or under the tail.

But they ran away then, because the second bull had decided to charge too.

It shook the earth, and it screamed through its up-lifted proboscis.

Gribardsun's spear had been snapped off when the beast fell on it. He had only a stone axe, which he took from his belt and threw. But it might as well have been made of feathers. It rotated through the air and its head struck the animal in the open mouth. It bounced out, and now the mammoth was concentrating on him.

He turned and ran. As he did so, he looked for von Billmann, who had been on the left with the rifle. He could see nothing of him and had not time to speculate where he was.

Though Gribardsun was very fast, he was not as swift as the mammoth. Its long legs covered the ground faster than his could, and suddenly the trumpeting and thundering of the hoofs was close behind him. With a yell he leaped to one side, and the mammoth reared up and whirled around with an unbelievable, and terrifying, swiftness.

Gribardsun ran forward and through the front legs

of the startled creature and then threw himself to one side.

The mammoth whirled around him, stopped, and reversed its horizontal rotation on seeing the man rolling away.

Angrogrim, yelling, ran in past Gribardsun and hurled his spear into the open mouth of the beast. Its point disappeared into the pinkish flesh.

Gribardsun leaped up and ran off with the mammoth again pursuing him. Shivkaet launched a spear from his atlatl not ten feet from the beast, and the shaft drove at least a foot into its side.

The mammoth, however, would not be turned aside. It had its heart set on trampling Gribardsun.

The Englishman looked to his right. The tribesmen were running toward them with the intention of hurling their spears at the beast. Beyond, Drummond was looking through the camera's viewfinder. He was carrying a .32-caliber rifle with explosive bullets, but he seemed intent only on getting good pictures.

The yelling hunters swarmed in and the spears flew. One scraped Gribardsun's shoulder and another plunged into the ground and he had to leap over it.

But a series of thuds told him that many had plunged into the mammoth. He looked behind him; the beast had slowed down. Half a dozen shafts were sticking out from its sides, and one had entered a few inches into its right front leg and lamed it.

Then the express rifle boomed out three times, and the beast, gouting blood from great holes in its side, fell over. The impact made the earth quiver under Gribardsun's naked feet.

Drummond, his rifle still suspended on a strap over his shoulder, walked up and circled the beast, his camera taking in all the details.

Von Billmann, looking distressed, ran up to the Englishman.

"I'm sorry I didn't shoot sooner," he said. "But I caught my heel on a rock and fell on my head. I was stunned for a minute or so."

He brushed the back of his head and showed Gribardsun the blood still welling from the cut.

Silverstein did not comment.

The Englishman said, "I realize the necessity of taking films. But didn't you understand that I was in bad trouble?"

Silverstein flushed and said, "No, I didn't. By the time I realized that von Billmann should be shooting, it was too late. And then things happened so fast that I froze. But Robert did shoot then, and everything seemed all right."

"In the future, the cameraman will have to be a backup for the rifleman," Gribardsun said. "An alert backup." He turned away. There was nothing more to say. Silverstein was an intelligent man and would realize what Gribardsun could have said. Gribardsun was not sure that Silverstein had frozen because of panic. He might have been hoping, consciously or unconsciously, that the mammoth would trample Gribardsun.

The Englishman waved away the tribesmen who wanted to smear his forehead with the mammoth's blood. He sterilized the cut on the German's head and sprayed it with pseudoskin. Then he accepted the mammoth's tail and permitted the daubing.

The rest of the day was heavy work. The beasts were cut up into pieces small enough to haul. The entire tribe, except for the sick and the very old, of whom there were few, helped carry the meat in.

While the work was going on, the vultures, ravens, wolves, and hyenas gathered around. Presently two cave lions appeared, scattered a pack of hyenas, and occupied their spot. They sat watching, occasionally roaring but not offering to approach closer. And then the hyenas suddenly attacked the lions.

Gribardsun shouted at Drummond to take pictures. This was too good to miss. There was nothing cowardly about these great beasts, and their teamwork was worthy of wolves. One would dash in and snap at a lion, and when the lion whirled and leaped, another would run in behind him and bite. Every time a lion bounded after a fleeing hyena, he had to quit chasing it because of painful bites on his tail or rear legs.

But a hyena was caught and killed by one of the lions as it tormented the other. Before it died, the hyena bit down once and the immensely powerful jaws broke the lioness's right front leg. The lioness closed her jaws on the hyena's hindquarters and scooped out its entrails with a huge paw. But she was crippled thereafter, and her mate, a giant possibly a third larger than the African lions of Gribardsun's time, was hard put to it to defend her. He was of a beautiful golden color that reminded Gribardsun of a pet he had once had in Kenya. He lacked the mane of the African lion, however.

The people had stopped working on the mammoths when the uproar of the battle broke out. Thammash spoke to Gribardsun.

"Those lions may be the ones that killed Skrinq last year. It would be good if we made sure that the male is dead, too, and so revenge Skrinq. And also make life a bit safer for us."

"I think the hyenas will do your work for you," Gribardsun said.

The lion had just wheeled on a tormentor, and as he did so, the two who had been dancing just a few feet from him, ran in and seized a leg. They gave one bite and spun and raced away. The lion turned again, but he fell on his side. Though he got up immediately, it was evident that he was hamstrung in one leg.

"After the lion is dead, kill the hyenas," Thammash said. "We have lost more people, especially children, to the hyenas than to the lions."

"When I was a young man, I hated hyenas," Gribardsun said. "They seemed to me to be only cowardly stinking carrion eaters. But I came to know them better and to end up by admiring them. They are not cowardly, just intelligently cautious. They hunt quite often and bring down game. And they have affection for their cubs and can, if caught young and raised properly, be very intelligent and affectionate pets."

The idea of raising any animal as a pet—except for the bear cubs—boggled Thammash. But that anybody could admire hyenas almost staggered him.

The tormenting attacks lasted for about five minutes more. Then the lion was bowled over and he and about six hyenas became a rolling roaring cachinnating yelping mess. Two hyenas were killed and one was severely wounded. But the lion was dead, his windpipe crushed between a male's jaws.

The lioness was next, and she ripped the side off a hyena before she died. The survivors began eating at once, and the wolves and birds moved in closer, waiting for their chance. Thammash ordered some of his men to follow him in an effort to drive off the hyenas. He wanted the two heads and the tails. The rest the hyenas could have, since there was already so much meat harvested.

The hyenas retreated reluctantly but did not attack. The heads and tails were hacked off and brought back triumphantly.

"This has been a great day!" Thammash cried. "You have brought us much good fortune, Koorik!"

Thammash did not think the fortune was so good when the people moved on to the site of the dead rhinoceros. He and the three strangers and half of his tribe were moving across the plain to the rhinoceroses when they saw three men racing toward them.

Thammash ran out to meet them. Gribardsun followed. He was in time to hear Shimkoobt, a man of about forty, gasp out the end of his story.

While the six Wota'shaimg were cutting up one of the rhinos, they were attacked by fourteen Wotagrub. These sprang out from the heavy growth, yelling and throwing spears and boomerangs. Treekram had fallen with a spear sticking out of his thigh. The remaining five had thrown their spears without effect. The invaders had then thrown a second volley, and Lramg'bud had been hit in the neck with a heavy boomerang. The Wotagrub had then charged, and the four had turned and fled. But another boomerang struck Kwakamg on a leg and he fell down. Before he could get up, he was speared.

The news was a great shock. The loss of the meat was not so much, since they had two mammoths at the other site. But the loss of four men in one day was a terrible blow to the Wota'shaimg.

The women, on hearing the news, started to wail. Thammash told them to keep quiet and get back to their work. He detailed Angrogrim and Shivkaet to follow him and set off. Gribardsun and von Billmann went with him; Silverstein stayed behind to guard.

Gribardsun had wondered for only a few seconds why the chief took only two men with him against the invaders. But then he saw that Thammash expected Gribardsun and von Billmann to use their magical weapons against the Wotagrum. The Englishman was now carrying the express rifle.

On seeing them at a distance of half a mile, however,

the Wotagrub ran off; but not without taking those parts of the rhinoceros which the Wota'shaimg had already cut off.

All of the bodies, including Trimk's, had been mutilated and the heads removed. Von Billmann took some films of these and then vomited.

Thammash stood silent for a long time. Then he spoke to Gribardsun.

"Shouldn't we go after them and kill them?"

Gribardsun did not reply at once. The deaths of the men had affected him, since he was coming to know them as individuals and even becoming fond of several. Moreover, if the killings were unpunished, the Wotagrub would try again. And if the tribe lost many more men, it would be in a critical situation.

However, he did not like to take on the powers of a god. He would have liked to stand to one side and study the relationships of the two tribes. Let them work out their own histories; if one perished, then that was too bad. But that was also the way things were.

And he also hoped to be able to make friends with the Wotagrub and study them. He could not do so if he killed their men.

"Once you're involved, you have to take a stand," he told von Billmann in English. "If we take the lives of their enemies, we'll become one of the Wota'shaimg. Literally, because I'm sure they'll adopt us. That is, if they have the custom of adoption."

He asked Thammash if the tribe ever made aliens members of their people.

Thammash said, "I have never heard of such a thing."

Evidently these people were not as advanced as, say, the North American Indian of pre-Columbian times.

"If you capture a baby," Gribardsun said, "what do you do with him? Kill him?"

Thammash's face brightened. He said, "No, of course not, if he is healthy. We raise him to be a warrior and a hunter. But that is different. A baby is not an enemy. Nor even a Wota'shaimg."

A Wota'shaimg was a human being. A non-Wota'-shaimg was not fully human.

"He becomes a Wota'shaimg when he goes through the initiation of manhood," Thammash said.

Gribardsun knew that he could not turn down the request for help. The relationship between the explorers and the tribe would never be the same again. And there was the strong urging of his own feelings to consider. He was outraged, and even touched by grief, at the death and the mutilation of his tribesmen.

His tribesmen! he thought.

He said, "Very well. We'll trail them."

And we'll see what happens then, he thought.

The four—Gribardsun, Thammash, von Billmann and Shivkaet—set out. They avoided ambush in the heavy growth by climbing above it on the hillside. Gribardsun thought it unlikely that the Wotagrub would dare to try an ambush, but there was no sense taking chances.

They trotted along swiftly but looked for tracks or other signs of the pursued. They found a few that led toward the overhang under which the Wotagrub lived. Rather, it was the overhang under which they *had* lived. When they cautiously approached the site, they found the tents gone and cold ashes in the hearths.

"They must have moved some time ago," Gribardsun said.

They cast about on all sides, including the hill above the overhang. But the frequent spring rains tended to wash out footprints and to carry off bits of fur caught on plants or dropped objects.

"Give me the .32 and its ammo," Gribardsun said

to von Billmann. "I'm going after those fellows, and I don't want to be held back by slow runners."

Von Billmann did as he was requested without protest. Gribardsun told the two tribesmen what he planned to do. They protested that they wanted to be in on the death. The Englishman refused to allow them to go with him.

"Your people need you," he said. "Now. Every hand available should be carrying the meat and the tusks of the beasts."

"You are a very strong man," Thammash said. "You could carry much meat."

Gribardsun smiled and said, "True. But it is more important that I convince the Wotagrub that they should leave us alone."

Von Billmann said, "I can see the necessity of ensuring that our subjects are protected so we can study them. But you shouldn't go alone."

"But I am," Gribardsun said. He ran off down the hillside and was soon lost to sight as he made his way back up the hill to the top.

The two tribesmen poked around the camp for anything of value the enemy might have left behind. And then the three departed.

Chapter 3

Rachel Silverstein was very disturbed by the account of the hunt, Gribardsun's narrow escape, and the killings and mutilations. But she was most upset by the report of his lone expedition.

"Why did you let him go?"

Von Billmann shrugged and said, "I'm not strong enough to force him to return. Besides, he *is* the leader."

"But he's out alone in that savage wilderness! Anything could happen to him! We might never see him again, not even know what happened!"

"That's true," von Billmann said. "And he knows it. But I'm not worried. Not much, anyway. He can take care of himself. If anybody can, he can. Would you like to see the films of the hunt? You'll see what I mean then."

Drummond Silverstein said, "Rachel, if I had gone, would you be as concerned?"

Von Billmann, embarrassed, walked away. He looked back a moment later and saw them face to face, their skins flushed and their mouths writhing.

The last of the carcasses was brought in after dusk. Everybody except the babies went to bed very late that night. They cooked a great quantity of the meat and ate with good appetite, despite the wails and tears of the mourning women and children. Some of these ate greedily between fits of grief. And racks of wood were prepared and meat placed over them to be smoked. The meat was scraped off the rhino skulls, which were then broken open so that the brains could be cut out. The skulls were later placed in holes in the ground and filled with water. Heated stones were dropped in, and the pieces of meat left on the skulls were boiled free to make soup.

Rachel talked to some of the widows. Their lot was not to be a happy one, not that it had been enviable when their mates were still alive. They would become the secondary wives of the most important men in the community, if they were still of childbearing age. They would be under the authority of the first wives. They and their children would always get what was left over in the way of food or attention. This would be more than enough when times were good. The tribe did not want widows and orphans to suffer needlessly. But when meat was scarce, the first wives and their children would get first choice.

On the other hand, the high death rate among females of childbearing age gave the secondary wives a chance to become first.

Life was hard and insecure for everybody.

Four days went by. The three fretted. Rachel and Drummond hardly spoke to each other until the morning of the fourth. Then they became civil and kissed each other good morning. Apparently they had had some form of reconciliation that night, though probably not until after some verbal violence.

Von Billmann said, "Too much time has gone by. I'm going out to look for him tomorrow. Would you two want to come along?"

"Of course we will," Rachel said.

"He should have taken along a radio," Drummond said. "His idea of going native was stupid. He could at least have taken a radio and we'd know where he was and if he was all right."

"It was stupid of us not to think of it," von Billmann said. "But I was too excited, and he just doesn't think about such things as keeping people informed of his whereabouts. He's a strange man, no doubt of that. There's something very peculiar about his being picked to go on this expedition, you know. Almost sinister, though I hate to say that about Gribardsun."

"I would think so!" Rachel said. She made no attempt to hide her anger. "How can you say anything bad about him? What's he done? Let's hear it!"

"Your emotions are showing," Drummond said in a dull voice.

"Why shouldn't they?" she said. "Isn't it natural for me to get upset if anyone of us should be missing? Isn't it right?"

"I'm sorry I said anything," he replied.

"What did you mean, almost sinister?" Rachel said to von Billmann. "And why is there anything strange about his being chosen? He's certainly qualified, isn't he?"

"I don't think there's any doubt about that *now*," von Billmann said. "But when the expedition was first proposed, de Longnors was the outstanding candidate as the leader. He was a brilliant medical doctor, both as diagnostician and researcher. He also had written many outstanding—some of them classic—works on physical anthropology, and he had done brilliant work as an archeologist and botanist. He was just the type of man needed, one who could carry out superb research in a number of fields."

"I had heard that he was considered," Drummond

said. "But I thought that he was finally rejected because he was too hard to get along with."

"That did go against him, but nobody else had his brilliance. John Gribardsun was one of the other candidates considered. He had the same versatile background as de Longnors but he had not been famous in any of them. He had published very little, and his medical practice was limited to taking care of the natives on the Inner Kenyan Sanctuary, where he lived so many years. But then the name of Gribardsun was heard more and more often in the news media and the guest shows. And he appeared on various guest panels, you know, and charmed his audience."

"Hypnotized them, you mean," Drummond said.

"In a way perhaps; he does have some curiously magnetic quality," von Billmann said. "Anyway," he went on, "we people interested in the project, in the know about the scene behind the curtains, you might say, soon found out that he was being considered as de Longnors' backup. There were other men even more qualified who had been bypassed."

"How do you know they were more qualified?" Rachel said.

"The project executives thought so," von Billman said. "At first, anyway. I was told that the test ratings indicated Gribardsun was about sixth on the list. But, suddenly, he was second. There was a good deal of talk about that. Some people thought Gribardsun must have found out something about some of the top executives, or some of the politicians connected with the project, and was blackmailing them."

"That's a terrible thing to say!" Rachel said. "How could anybody believe it?"

"You know how people are," von Billmann said. "You'll have to admit that it *was* mysterious. It's *still* mysterious. Though there's no doubt in my mind that the right man was chosen. The question is, were the right methods used to pick him? Or, rather, did he use the proper channels and procedures to get chosen?"

"Did he?" Rachel said.

Von Billmann shrugged and said, "I do not know. It was all so odd and so sudden. De Longnors disappears . . . "

"We knew about that, of course," Drummond said.

"And after a while the executives announce that John Gribardsun has been chosen to take his place. Then, a week later, de Longnors is found wandering on the seventh level of Center Paris. He is incoherent and suffering from amnesia. He recovers somewhat in that he remembers everything except the period of his disappearance. That is a blank. By then, the vessel was scheduled for launch. De Longnors had missed too much of the necessary training. Besides, he might be mentally unstable. So he was left behind."

Rachel was furious but controlling herself. She said, "Are you hinting that John might have had something to do with de Longnors' disappearance and his amnesia? That he was abducted and drugged?"

"No, I'm not hinting that John had anything to do with it. As you must know by now, I have nothing but the greatest admiration for John Gribardsun. I'm glad that he, and not de Longnors, was picked. All I'm saying is that something strange was going on at the time. And that, a year before the vessel was launched, John Gribardsun had little chance of being on it.

"It's a tremendously important thing to be chosen as one of the crew of the *H. G. Wells I*," von Billmann continued. "This is a unique voyage. There will be other trips into time, but none this far back again. We are indeed fortunate. I've thanked whatever gods there are that I was one of the four chosen out of thousands who qualified. And that brings up another thing. John once told me that he started training for this trip over twenty years ago, when it was first proposed that the theory of time travel might be made a reality. He was already a cultural anthropologist; he had a Ph.D., though he had never taught. So he figured out what type of man would be needed on an expedition into the past, and he became an M.D., and then got a doctor's degree in archeology and botany and several master's degrees in related fields.

"Now, a man that determined to get a berth on the time ship, one who sets out twenty years before it is established that there will be a ship—that man isn't going to let a kidnapping and a drugging get in his way."

"You make me furious!" Rachel said. "First you tell us all these sinister bits of information. Then you say they're just guesses, and you worship Gribardsun, and then . . ."

"I admire and respect him very much. I didn't say anything about worshipping him. You must understand. I don't want to think any ill of John. I like him too much for that. But I am a scientist, and I have to consider certain theories. Especially when certain facts start to build up a certain picture. But nothing is proved anyway. Or probably ever will be."

"Well, I wouldn't blame him if he had played a dirty trick on de Longnors," Drummond said.

Rachel looked surprised. Her husband said, "Nor would I have blamed de Longnors if Gribardsun had been in his place and he was the one who did the abducting and drugging. The crew of the *H. G. Wells I* will be famous forever."

"I think that it won't be good to have this kept among us three," von Billmann said. "We should bring it out in the open; talk it over with Gribardsun. I

don't want you to think I'm talking behind his back.
Nor would I want him to think that. So why don't we
tell him about this conversation?"

"That would at least be honest," Rachel said.

"But not womanly," Drummond said.

'What do you mean by that?"

"Just a thought," Drummond said. "It doesn't apply
to you, of course, since you're so outspoken."

"I don't know," she said. "Perhaps we should re-
consider. If he felt that we suspected him of under-
handedness—of, in fact, criminal behavior—wouldn't
that make things difficult? It's bad enough as it is,
being forced into intimate contact for four years, never
seeing any other human beings. *Real* human beings, I
mean," she said, as von Billmann opened his mouth
to protest.

Drummond laughed.

"You know what I mean!" she said. *"Civilized* men,
then! People who think as we do! But, really, what
good will it do? You don't expect him to admit anything dishonest, do you? And what if he did? Or didn't,
for that matter? What then? What good would it do?
I've changed my mind. I think we ought to keep such
suspicions to ourselves."

"I don't," von Billmann said. "John isn't the kind
who likes festering secrets. He'd rather bring them out
in the open."

"I think it should be discussed," Drummond said,
looking strangely at Rachel.

The funeral rites took most of one day. The dead
men were placed side by side in a single shallow
grave. They were placed on their right sides, knees
drawn up against their bellies and arms down their
sides, the fingers touching the ankles. They were clad
in full skin suits, their necks hung with chains of per-

forated stones and pierced bear teeth and claws. Their stone and wooden weapons were placed beside them and pieces of mammoth and rhino meat were placed near the mouths. The bodies were then covered with bearskins and more bear teeth strewn over the skins. Dirt was piled over the skins while the widows and their children, along with Thrimk's parents, circled the grave widdershins. They wailed and wept and beat their breasts with their fists and sometimes called on Wota'aimgkrimq, the Great She-Bear. Later, Rachel would ask them what they thought about the afterlife. But they, like the civilized and savage people of the time-travelers' own period, had only a vague and often contradictory concept of what happened after they died.

The adult men and women then piled rocks on top of the dirt until there was enough to discourage bears and hyenas from digging them up. Glamug danced around shaking a baton and chanting from behind his bear mask. When the last rock was piled on, the tribe walked slowly back to the shelf under the overhang. And there they had a big feast.

The scientists stood around at a respectful distance and filmed the entire ceremony.

On the way home that evening, Rachel said, "I wonder what happened to that burial site? I know that very spot was dug up sometime in 1980, and nothing was found there."

Drummond shrugged and said, "I suppose very few graves survived. They were dug up eventually by animals or washed away. And many must have been removed during the building of houses and other constructions in the early days when people didn't pay much attention to such things. And, of course, there must be thousands of burial sites which just haven't been discovered yet because there was no apparent reason to dig. In any case nothing but the stone implements and beads would remain."

"When we get back, I'm going to look this spot over," Rachel said. "There might be something they overlooked, even if it's only a fossilized bear tooth or a flint spear head."

"A lot can happen in 14,000 years," he said.

Two more days passed. Rachel fretted until she got on Drummond's nerves. He told her to quit worrying, or at least keep it to herself. And he added that he doubted that she would worry as much if he were gone that long. This led to another quarrel, which they tried, unsuccessfully, to keep from von Billmann, who guessed its origin correctly. He said nothing to either of them; he did not care to get involved, especially in an affair which he disapproved of. They were scientists and so should have left their less worthy emotions behind them in A.D. 2070. He could understand why Rachel had fallen for Gribardsun, since he did in fact, despite his earlier protestation to her, come as close to worshipping the man as he would allow himself to. But she should repress her feelings and not permit them to interfere with their work.

He did not tell them this, of course. But they knew him well; they could almost read his thoughts.

On the fifth day, John Gribardsun walked into camp. With him he brought two strangers.

At a distance, his colleagues would have had trouble recognizing him if he had not still been clean-shaven.

His two companions were almost as tall as Gribardsun and fully as broad-shouldered. One had reddish hair and the other yellow-brown. Their eyes were blue. Their bones were large, and their supraorbital ridges were prominent. Though they were Caucasian, they had slight epicanthic folds, indicating, perhaps, some Mongolian genes.

Gribardsun strode into camp as if he owned it which, in a sense, he did. The strangers hung back until he turned and gestured for them to join him. They put their spears and atlatls and boomerangs on the ground and climbed up to the ledge. Their wooden-handled flint knives were still in their sheaths, however.

Gribardsun introduced them as Klhmnhach and Rhtinhlhk. They smiled nervously and spoke in a strange whispering speech.

Von Billmann, hearing them, smiled so broadly that his face threatened to split. Gribardsun laughed and said, "Their language is a linguist's delight, Robert. Very few vowels and most of the consonants are unvoiced. And nothing like anything ever recorded in Europe."

The Bear People did not like the strangers at all. Thammash protested loudly while he made threatening gestures at the two. They moved closer together, but their faces remained expressionless and their fingers were widespread.

There was a brief interruption when Laminak, Dubhab's pre-teenaged daughter, ran to Gribardsun and threw her arms around his waist and hugged him while she wept. The Englishman patted her head and murmured something about being happy to see her again. Then he gently pushed her away, and her mother took her hand and led her away while she scolded her.

"You've made another conquest," Rachel said. Her smile was hard.

Gribardsun did not reply. He addressed the entire tribe, telling them that he had made peace with the strangers, the Wotagrub, whose name for themselves was *Krhshmhnhik*. This meant The People. The tribesmen were unable to pronounce the word anywhere near correctly, nor would they make much of an effort. For them, the Krhshmnhik remained the Wotagrub.

Gribardsun did not say how he had talked the Wota-grub into making peace. Nor did he say anything about taking revenge for their having killed so many Wota'-shaimg. From now on there would be peace. The Wota-grub would move even farther away. The borders of the two tribes would be such and such, and he defined them as exactly as he could, using landmarks both tribes knew well. If one tribesman ventured into the territory of the other tribe, he must refrain from hunting there.

The Wota'shaimg did not like anything he said. They wanted an eye for an eye. In fact, two eyes for an eye. And they could not understand why such a powerful magician and warrior as Gribardsun did not exact vengeance.

The Englishman explained that he could have wiped out the whole tribe easily. But he saw no reason to do so. That was that.

He later told his colleagues that it would have done no good to have gone into ethics or morality. The Wota'shaimg would not have understood his modern philosophy. The best thing to do was to issue an edict as if he were a god. They could understand that. If they did not understand rationality, they understood power. The great magician and wicked warrior—to them, wicked was a compliment—required such and such or would punish them. So they would do as he said, even if they did not like it.

Gribardsun ordered a feast, and the two strangers squatted with the elders of the tribe and the scientists and ate with them. After that, they relaxed. The Wota'-shaimg were not likely to murder them if they ate with them. The sharing of food implied safety for those who shared. There was no spoken law to this effect. It was just understood.

The time travelers examined the boomerangs of the

strangers. These were carved with flint and consisted of a heavy close-grained wood which they could not identify as yet. The wood did not grow in this area. Gribardsun said he could speak only a few words— word-sentences, rather—of the strangers. But through sign language he had learned that their origin was far to the south, and that they had brought these boomerangs from their native territory. That was probably either in southern Iberia or possibly North Africa. The two would be connected with a land bridge, of course, since the Mediterranean Sea was much smaller and lower now. The Wotagrub had once had many boomerangs, but they had been in this country so long that they had lost most of them. And there was no wood appropriate for making new ones.

"I believe that a trip southward, say about the time fall is due, would be consistent with our purpose," Gribardsun said. He chewed on a piece of rare-cooked ibex steak for a moment and then said, "We could travel swiftly to get away from the effects of winter here. Winter farther south won't be so severe that we can't travel. And I think we should take a look at the land bridge and at North Africa."

"Isn't that rather dangerous, putting ourselves so far away from our vessel?" Drummond said. "I admit the scientific desirability of studying the southern area. But we must weigh the possible results against the chances of killing ourselves off and so ruining the entire expedition. After all, the power spent on getting us here and back, and the fact that this is absolutely the only chance we'll get for a personal look into the Magdalenian period—well, I don't think we should get too far away from our base of operations. Here we have the situation well in hand. But if we wander around, just four of us, we're subject to attack, to acci-

dent, to many things. We might be cut off. We might
. . ."

"Anything that could happen south could happen
here," Gribardsun said. "Let's think about it. We have
a month before autumn comes. We'll consider the feas-
ibility of austral explorations then."

"Meanwhile," von Billmann said, "I'd like to record
the language of the Wotagrub. Do you think it would
be all right if I returned with these two?"

"Why not?" Gribardsun said. "But I'd like you to
collect some animal specimens, too, including entomo-
logical specimens, if you could. And get samples of
the blood of the Wotagrub if you can. Don't push too
hard at first about that, though."

The German was delighted.

He stood up and said, "I'll get my tent and recorder
and other equipment and leave as soon as possible."

"Sometime tomorrow," Gribardsun said, smiling.
"We have some things to thresh out, a policy to determine regarding the Wotagrub. It's necessary that
everybody understand exactly where we stand. And
that won't be easy, since we have to communicate
with the Wotagrub through signs."

It was late when the fires were allowed to dim and
the time travelers, the elders, and the two strangers
went to bed. But Gribardsun was satisfied that everybody understood, in general, what the relationship
of the two tribes was to be.

The following afternoon, von Billmann, carrying a
large pack on the duraluminum rack on his back,
walked off with the two strangers. They also carried
packs, the German's equipment and supplies. Von Billmann was exhilarated, and he joked with his two
companions. They could not understand a word he

said, of course, but they understood his joy, and they smiled back at him.

Rachel, watching him march off between them, said, "Do you really think that it's wise to let him go off alone, John?"

He did not answer. He had a habit, annoying to her, of not answering questions if he thought they didn't deserve an answer.

Rachel bit her lip and looked at Drummond. He shrugged and moved away. He knew that she wanted him to give her moral support when she questioned Gribardsun about his past. But von Billmann had left them so suddenly that they felt weakened. It had been easy to talk about the questions they would ask Gribardsun when he returned. But now that he was here, he seemed formidable. He would doubtless resent their questions and refuse to answer them. And even if he did, then what? The fact was, they were all here together and they must all work together. In any case, Rachel did not credit a word of their absurd suspicions that Gribardsun had somehow got on the expedition through foul play.

Drummond had asked her how she *knew*. Did she really know the Englishman that well?

Rachel had admitted that she did not, certainly not in any sense that Drummond may have implied. But her feminine intuition, her perceptivity, irrational perhaps but nevertheless valid, told her that Gribardsun was not a felon or a maniac. She knew he was a decent human being, just as a moth knows that certain flying objects are not bats. But her antennae were invisible.

Drummond had laughed at that and asked her how in the world she had ever gotten her doctorate in zoology. Angrily, she had replied that perhaps he was right about her intuitions. They had told her that

Drummond was a strong man, a good husband, and that he was in love with her. But she had been mistaken. So perhaps her intuitions about Gribardsun were also wrong.

Drummond had then become angry in turn, and they had quarreled again.

Chapter 4

The summer passed swiftly, and the short autumn
of the glacial age was upon them. Gribardsun had by
then apparently given up the idea, at least temporarily,
of traveling to the south. There was so much to be
done in this little area that it would have seemed shirk-
ing their duties to travel elsewhere.

Gribardsun's study of the Wota'shaimg language
had so far revealed a vocabulary of more "words"
than he would have expected. He was convinced that
there were at least that many more. Although it was a
poor language for communicating intellectual ideas,
it was surprisingly versatile in words for emotions, sen-
sations and impressions. And, it had a highly technical
language for those things most important to the Wota'-
shaimg: hunting, fishing, various types of animals and
stone, shades of lights, kinds of snow and ice.

Their numeral system went up to twenty, and past
that they used the word for "many." But they could
describe exactly each member of a group exceeding
the number of twenty, some of them being able to list
with all necessary distinguishing features each bison
of a herd of forty.

They all had a phenomenal ability for reciting long

tales and certain common magical formulae. Wazwim, the singer, could chant four thousand lines of a poem without prompting. He did this three times over a period of two months for Gribardsun, and his lines seldom varied. However, whenever he thought of an improvement, he would promptly make it then and there.

The chant was only roughly a poem. The feet were based on quantity, though far removed from the classical Latin or Greek quantity. The line was roughly composed of a sort of trochaic hexameter. There was no rhyme but much alliteration.

Nor could the poem be called an epic in the true sense of the word. It was a loose collection of narratives of heroes and totem animals and evil spirits intermixed with magical formulae and folk wisdom. The closest parallel to the "epics" that modern man knew was the Finnish *Kalevala*. Everything had taken place long long ago, starting in fact, before the creation of the universe and continuing up until a dozen generations ago, when the last of the heroes had died. Men today were only ordinary men, according to the song, weaklings and poor-spirited. They didn't make men like they did in the old days.

Gribardsun was surprised that such a small, technologically retarded society could have produced such a relatively sophisticated poem; and with, for all its serviceable flexibility, a nonetheless essentially primitive vocabulary. Its existence in such a society went against all that he knew and had been taught. He said as much.

"That's the frustrating thing about the limitations on time travel," Drummond said. "We can't go even farther back to check out the origin and the development of the so-called epic. Or of anything."

Gribardsun nodded, but he did not seem too unhappy about it. It was obvious that he was, in fact, very happy. He went out hunting with the others, or sometimes alone, and he always came back with meat. He seldom used his modern weapons but confined himself to using the tribal ones. He broke his own rule only when a big animal charged and made it necessary to use a rifle. Or when he went bird hunting. There were enormous flocks of ducks and geese settled around the lakes, and he went out happily dawn after dawn to hunt these. At first he killed them with a small spear or stones from a sling, or trapped them. But he occasionally took a shotgun and brought down dozens in one day.

"This is a paradise!" he said one evening to the Silversteins. "A world such as it should be! Damned few humans, and an abundance of wild life! And yet this place is barren compared to what Africa must be! We must go down there when spring comes!"

Drummond sometimes felt like remonstrating with Gribardsun. He thought that the Englishman spent too much time hunting when he should have been doing his scientific work. But Rachel said that he was learning the inner intimate life of the tribe by participating in their activities—not just by observations. Moreover, could Drummond truthfully say that Gribardsun had neglected any of his scientific work?

Every second day, von Billmann reported via their tiny transceivers. By the time the first snows came, he had recorded and noted enough of the language to keep him busy for years. He had also succeeded in gaining some fluency in the strange whispering speech.

"I'll be coming tomorrow," he said. "Leaving here, that is. They're giving a big shindig for me tonight. We'll be eating mammoth and bison and horse meat, lots of duck, and plenty of berries and greens. And that fermented berry and fruit juice I told you about. It tastes like hell, but it sure packs a punch."

That was another unexpected discovery. It had not been suspected that alcohol had been made so early. But the knowledge of alcohol was apparently not extensive as yet. The Wota'shaimg, for instance, knew nothing of it.

The main reason that von Billmann was returning, aside from his longing for civilized companionship, was that the Wotagrub were moving out.

This was another discovery that went against the supposed facts. It had been assumed that they roamed during the warm seasons and holed up in caves or under overhangs during the winter. The arctic winters of middle Europe were surely too harsh to permit much movement by humans.

But the Eskimos traveled over the arctic ice and lived off it during the winter. They were integrated with their environment. They had all the technology needed to enable them to cope with it. And so had the Magdalenians.

Sometimes, the tribes did hole up in one place all winter, if there was enough game in the area to support them. But when the game became scarce, the tribe packed its tents and belongings and went wherever the herds went. The game was getting scarce around here, partly because of the strangers' magical weapons. Everybody had eaten very well indeed, and fewer babies had died. But the big animals, the mammoths and the rhinos, had been scared out. They were becoming scarcer every year, anyway. The bison and the horses had moved on to some other area. The ibex were scarce for some reason. Even the great predators, the cave bear and the cave lion, had been killed or decided that the area was unsafe for them. And the reindeer had cropped up all the lichen and fungi and moved on.

Gribardsun solved the conflicting problems of remaining with the tribe to study them intensively and of exploring the land to the south.

Knowing that the tribesmen talked much among themselves of their dreams, and that they depended much on Glamug to interpret their dreams for them, Gribardsun planted the idea of going south. He described how much easier life would be where the snows weren't so deep, and soon some people did dream of traveling far south. They discussed these dreams among themselves and then went to Glamug with them.

Several had dreamed that Gribardsun led them south. Since the dreams were obviously wishes, and since they felt protected and provided for under Gribardsun, they wished him to conduct them into the paradise.

Glamug came to the Englishman and told him of what his people had dreamed. Gribardsun agreed with Glamug's analysis. Yes, he would be happy to guide them into the unknown lands to the south. They should start as soon as the long gray vessel was hauled up to the top of the hill and secured.

The ground was frozen, and a thin coat of ice had covered it after a partial snow. Even though they had gotten over most of their awe of the travelers themselves—though they retained all the original respect—they had never approached the vessel. Now, under Gribardsun's urgings, they poled over the vessel until they had it on wooden and bone sleds. Ivory and bone wedges were driven into the slots on top of the sleds to keep the vessel from rolling off.

Meanwhile, other workers had chopped with reindeer antler picks through the ice and into the frozen earth. Stakes were driven into the holes. The long rawhide ropes were attached to the sleds and the other ends run several times around the stakes. The tribe, digging in their boots into the chopped-out steps along the slide, heaved on the ropes. The sleds and their three-hundred-ton burden moved slowly, oh, so slowly, upward.

It took until past dusk to get the *H. G. Wells I* over the crest of the steep hill. The work was carried on by burning pine torches and by lights set up by the travelers. The air was cold; the breaths steamed; and their sweat froze on their faces and on their beards. But they had eaten well, and Rachel had made gallons of hot cocoa, which the tribe tasted for the first time and could not get enough of. Gribardsun kept up a stream of jokes and worked alongside them, pitting himself against Angrogrim, who tried to show that he was not only as big as a horse but as strong as one.

By ten o'clock that night, without the death or injury of a single person, they had restored the vessel to its original position. Large boulders were rolled alongside to keep it from moving in any direction.

"There's nothing to keep some wandering tribe from rolling it down again if they want to go to the trouble," Gribardsun said. "But I doubt that anybody will touch it. It's too frighteningly alien for these people."

The following morning was bright and clear, though cold. The tribe packed their tents and other artifacts and piled them on travois-like poles. These had broad ends, somewhat like skis, which slid over the snow without sinking much. The women and the juvenile males pulled the travois while the men spread out ahead, behind, and on the flanks as guards. They all sang the Going-Away Song, taking farewell of the place which had protected them for three seasons and to which they would return—if they were fortunate.

They also sang the Song of Shimg'gaimq, a legendary hero who had led the tribe from the far south in the far past. At the end of the song they substituted

Gribardsun's name for Shim'gaimq; the implication was that he was a new hero and even greater than the old.

The trek southward was slow. Heavy snows began to fall, and there were days when they could do nothing but hole up. Rachel and Drummond tended to stay huddled up inside their foam hut, which had been transported on skis. Gribardsun and von Billmann went out with the hunters, and they used their rifles. To have restricted themselves to native weapons might have meant that the tribe would starve, or at least go very hungry for some time. The game just seemed to have disappeared. Yet they knew that the deep snows hid plenty of bison and reindeer. The behemoth mammoths and rhinoceroses should also be somewhere around, penned in by high walls of snow. If they could be located, they could be speared with little chance of their escaping.

Gribardsun finally located a "yard" which held a herd of thirty bison. He shot three males, and they butchered them while the other bulls pawed the snow-streaked grasses and snorted and made rumbling noises. But none charged, and presently the carcasses of the bulls were hauled away in many pieces. Then the big gray wolves appeared and devoured what the men had left behind. The last Gribardsun saw of them, they were slinking toward the herd. He doubted that they would dare attack in the "yard" where the bulls had freedom of movement and the wolves could not get away swiftly.

The tribe ate for three days and then set out again. They continued through the deep snows, with frequent rest stops, until they came to the foothills of the Pyrenees. The passes of the range were blocked with snow and ice. The tribe could either camp until after the spring thaws—and much of the snow never melted even in the summer—or go around the mountains by way of the sea.

Here Gribardsun met his first serious resistance from the Wota'shaimg. They knew nothing of boats; they did not even know how to swim. When they learned what was expected of them, they refused. They would not set out on the ghastly gray seas even if they could stay close to the shore. The very idea paralyzed them with terror.

The travelers built a boat by hollowing out a log. (This far south there were some trees large enough to provide adequate trunks for dugouts.) The four worked energetically for three days, and on the fourth they launched the craft in the heavy-rolling bitterly cold surf of what would some day be called the Bay of Biscay. They paddled around for an hour to demonstrate to the tribe what could be done with a boat. Then they returned to the beach to still unconvinced observers. And that was all the people wanted to be: observers. Participation was unthinkable for them, or so they claimed.

There were only two exceptions. Angrogrim volunteered to accompany them, since he felt that his reputation for courage must be upheld. The other was Laminak, who said she would go wherever Gribardsun went.

The Englishman seized on this chance to hold up the others to scorn. Were they fearful to go where a twelve-year-old *girl* dared to go? Were the men of the Wota'shaimg really less brave than a girl-child?

Gribardsun pressed this line and finally said that he would make up a song about the cowardly warriors of the Bear People if they did not show some guts very quickly. And so the men, and then the women, reluctantly agreed to build boats and set out along the coast. But it was two weeks before the people were able to handle the craft well enough, and several times a boat was capsized and the paddlers dumped. Three caught pneumonia but were brought quickly back to health with Gribardsun's medicine. Every person wore an inflatable preserver around their waist. These had been brought from the time vessel stores. There were so many in the stores because Gribardsun thought they might come in handy if supplies and specimens were to be hauled by boat at any time. The floaters could support large heavy containers if they should chance to get dumped into the water. In the meantime some were used as stabilizers on the primitive craft.

The fleet of ten large dugouts left the shores of what would some day be Gaul, and then France, and the boats, staying close to the shore, crept around the northern edge of the Iberian Peninsula. Near what would be the site of Lisbon, the boats put in for the last time and were dragged inshore and hidden. The Bear People were much relieved; at no time had they become fond of sea life, and they hoped never to have to endure it again.

Gribardsun led them across the peninsula, angling southeastward most of the time. They crossed great plains and went through heavy forests. Here the animal life was somewhat different; red deer and wild pigs were numerous, and there were many shaggy forest horses. But there were also great brown mountains of bison and woolly rhinos and mammoths, though these were not as numerous as on the other side of the Pyrenees. Conditions were changing, and within a thousand years or perhaps even less, the behemoths would be extinct in Iberia. The forest elephant was replacing them.

The cave bear and lion and hyena were numerous enough to require caution in hunting. And the tribesmen of Iberia were as hostile as their northern kinsmen. These, however, were easily dispersed with a few shots fired into the air or, if they persisted, were routed with a few hypodermic missiles containing a drug. The missiles were not harmless; they struck with considerable impact and left great painful bruises and sometimes broke ribs or arms. But they did not kill except once, when a hostile warrior, allergic to the drug, died in a seizure a few minutes after being shot.

Gribardsun dissected the corpse thoroughly, taking photographs of every organ, analyzing the blood and other tissues and studying the genetic structure. In the meantime, von Billmann recorded the speech of three prisoners. By the time they were released, they had supplied him with a basic grammar and about six thousand vocabulary items. One of the prisoners, however, died a few hours before his fellows were given their freedom. He seemed to have nothing outwardly wrong with him; he just gave up the ghost and died. Gribardsun thought that the death was the result of an alarm syndrome. His dissection confirmed his diagnosis. The man had gone into a shock from which he could not recover. He had been terrified from the time he woke up to find himself in the hands of alien peoples. And he had, unfortunately, seen Gribardsun carry off parts of the first dissection into the woods where he left them for the wolves to eat. He expected a similar fate, no doubt.

Von Billmann, however, was rejoicing. He was sure that his prisoners spoke a language which just might be the ancestor, or collateral ancestor, of Basque speech. It would be impossible to confirm it until the scientists made an extensive study after the vessel returned. In addition, of course, the evidence collected by the next expedition, planned for 8000 B.C., would have to be compared with von Billmann's. The glottochronology of a language over many thousands of years would show a considerable change. In fact, the stages of most languages separated by three thousand years would look like two entirely unrelated tongues to the layman and, indeed, to all but the most astute linguists. There were some tongues that resisted change more than others, such as Lithuanian and Russian; the stages of these did not show nearly as much mutation as, say, that between vulgar Latin and modern French.

But 12,000 years changed any language so much that the untutored would doubt that there was any relationship among the various branches which had evolved from it. Thus, the nonlinguist finds it difficult to believe that English, Russian, and Hindustani sprang from the same parent tongue. And the parent was only 3,500 years old. How much more degeneration in 12,-000 years?

"The theory, which is entirely unbacked by evidence, is that the Basque tongues of our day are the last descendants of a vast superfamily which once existed all over Europe and perhaps in North Africa and parts of Asia," Robert said. "But the rise of Indo-Hittite speakers swept away most of the Ur-Basque speakers. A small group, or small groups, of Indo-Hittites in the area near the Elbe River expanded. And through conquest and absorption imposed their dialects on other areas. And these changed, in time, to become the parents of the Germanic, Slavic, Baltic, Italic, Hellenic, Hittite, Tocharian, Armenian and Indic tongues, and God knows what others that history does not record. That is why I am so eager to go to that area and determine if I can find languages which could be pre-Indo-Hittite. Then the expedition in 8000 B.C. can get later specimens. Then we can establish some sort of glottochronology!"

Von Billmann paced back and forth while his whole being glowed. His love for ancient languages was far more passionate, and enduring than any he could have had for a woman. Or so it seemed to Rachel who, however, was given to exaggeration.

Von Billmann admitted that there were probably just as many tribes in France, and perhaps in any section of Europe, which used the pre-Basque languages, as there were in Iberia. But since one had been found here—or at least one had been found which might be pre-Basque—then it was likely that there were others in this area. Therefore, more speakers should be captured.

There was an ethical point to consider in his proposal. It was one thing to drug and capture men who attacked. But did the scientists have the right to track down human beings and imprison them even if it was only for a while? And for the sake of science, of course?

Gribardsun said that they had only four years here, and that their time was so limited that they could make only a spot check here and there. They could not resolve the existence of widespread pre-Basque speech if they were overly scrupulous about the aborigines' "rights." He meant to get specimens. After all, they would be treated well, and he would load them down with meat when he released them.

Rachel objected. She said that one man had died of shock just from being imprisoned. It was likely that what had happened once would happen again.

"That was only because I wasn't prepared for such an event," the Englishman said. "I have the drugs to counteract shock, and at the first symptom of an alarm syndrome, I'll use the drugs."

Rachel did not like it, but she gave in. Drummond said that these people would all be dead in a short time anyway, and that the benefits to science overrode any small inconvenience the aborigines might have.

"Would you say that if some time traveler from A.D. 3000 put you in a cage for scientific study?" Rachel said.

"Sure I would. I might not like the practice, but I would never refute the theory."

Gribardsun, von Billmann, Angrogrim, and Dubhab went hunting for "specimens." They found a young woman and her two children carrying firewood. Gribardsun hesitated; he did not want to frighten children.

"If we start discrimination, we'll end up not taking any specimens," von Billmann said. "But then that may be the best thing."

He was evidently having second thoughts.

"The woman may have a baby which is being taken care of temporarily by a neighbor or an old woman," the Englishman said.

"The children will be horribly frightened," von Billmann said.

Gribardsun smiled, shrugged, and stepped out from behind the big rock. The woman saw him first. Screaming, she dropped her firewood, grabbed her children's hands, forcing them to drop their wood, and ran away. The four men followed her slowly, and by the time they reached the camp, they were confronted by a dozen armed warriors, howling defiance and shaking spears and stone axes.

Establishing peaceful relations with this tribe took time, of course. But a display of two colorful and loud shots from a Very gun quietened them down. Gribardsun approached them making signs of peace. It so happened that none of his signs agreed with theirs, but they understood the intent back of them. And though it took three days before the travelers could approach a tribesman without the person beginning to shake and to edge away, the time spent was well worth it. Now, instead of only several terrified prisoners, the scientists had an entire tribe to study. They stayed on good terms by a display of magic tricks and by shooting several bison and holding a great feast afterward.

Their own tribe finally overcame their suspicious hostility and mingled with the other for a while. But this put such a strain on everybody that Gribardsun requested the Wota'shaimg to stay away from the strangers.

Von Billmann was happy because he had a new language but unhappy because it seemed to be totally unrelated to his pre-Basque specimen.

After two weeks, the scientists led the Wota'shaimg away. But they made contact with another tribe farther south, the largest unit encountered so far. This consisted of eighty individuals, and they used hardwood boomerangs. Moreover, their speech was obviously related to the Wotagrub of the north. Von Billmann settled down for a three-weeks recording and interview session. At the end of that time, the two groups said farewell at a big feast of horse and ibex meat, most of which was provided by Gribardsun's rifle.

It was during this time that the scientists began to have trouble with Dubhab.

Dubhab was a friendly man, usually smiling and joking. But behind the jesting was a determination to get all he could from everybody he met. Dubhab was the ancestor of all con men. And he was exceedingly ambitious. Unlike the others, he was not content with his position in the tribe. He might never have tried to move out of his place in the pecking order if the four strangers had not shown up. But from the beginning he had been very interested in the principles and operation of the firearms and the drugs and medicines.

Gribardsun had explained as well as he could within the technically limited vocabulary of the Wota'-shaimg. And he had permitted Dubhab to handle the firearms and to shoot animals several times.

This was a mistake. The other authorities, jealous, asked to use the guns. Gribardsun saw that it would not be good if the tribesmen overcame their awe of the thunder sticks, as they called them. They might actually try to seize them and turn them on the scientists, though this did not seem probable, since the tribesmen knew that the four strangers had many other resources. And they also regarded them as not quite human; as being, in essence, spirits in flesh.

Gribardsun denied the requests. He said that Dubhab had been allowed to handle the guns only to test his reaction to them. It was thought wiser not to let anybody else try them, and, furthermore, Dubhab would be denied their use from now on.

Dubhab smiled and said that whatever the strangers wished was his wish also. But Gribardsun wondered what was behind that smile and the big blue eyes. Dubhab continued to praise the charms of his older daughter Neliska and to say openly that Gribardsun should take her as a mate. There was no doubt that Dubhab hoped to profit from his position as father-in-law.

Neliska said that she would be honored to become Gribardsun's mate. Gribardsun said that Neliska was very desirable, but he had no plans for taking a mate for some time.

Dubhab then suggested, when he was alone with Gribardsun, that the Englishman take Neliska without benefit of the marriage ceremony. A great spirit such as Gribardsun would not be bound by the conventions that bound mere human beings. And Neliska would be happy to bear a child to the great spirit.

Gribardsun told Dubhab to shut up about this business or he would turn him in to the elders. And the elders might consider exiling Dubhab for even thinking of breaking the customs of the tribe.

Dubhab turned gray at this remark. Like all preliterates, he dreaded more than anything being cut off from his tribe. The mere suggestion turned his bones to ice.

Yet it was only two days later that he remarked to Gribardsun that a man equipped with firearms would be in a position to change the customs of the tribe.

"That man is not only the archetypal con man", Rachel said, "He is the Ur-Napoleon, the pre-Hitler type."

The Basic-Napoleon-cum-Confidence-Man, however, was begging Gribardsun a week later to pull one of his teeth. He was suddenly suffering excruciating pain from an impacted wisdom tooth. The Englishman used his tiny sonic machine to take pictures, and found that the tooth was deeply abscessed. Moreover, the other three teeth were rotten and would have to come out. And all three would fall apart during extractions; they would probably have to be dug out.

Gribardsun explained to Dubhab what he had to do. And he also made sure that Dubhab understood that he now owed his life to Gribardsun. If the teeth were left to natural processes, or to the brutal and inadequate oral surgery of Glamug, Dubhab would die. Gribardsun took such pains to establish Dubhab's debt of gratitude because he wanted to insure his behavior in the future.

The operation was a success, and the patient did not die, although there were times when he said he would almost rather be dead.

The entire tribe witnessed the operation. The most remarkable thing to them was that Dubhab slept through it.

Glamug asked for, and received, Dubhab's teeth,

which were mainly fragments. He put them into a little skin pouch, waved his one-eyed *baton de commandement* over it while he chanted protective phrases, and then buried them secretly on the side of a mountain under a rock. No one would be able to use them in magical rites against Dubhab. But Gribardsun suspected that Glamug kept several small pieces of a wisdom tooth in case Dubhab ever became hostile to him.

Then again, perhaps, Glamug was innocent. By custom, Dubham could kill him and go free if he caught Glamug using any parts of his body—nails, teeth, hairs, saliva—against him.

Dubhab recovered amazingly fast, helped by the antibiotics and Gribardsun's care. Three days later, the tribe packed their tents and belongings and moved southward again. Gribardsun marched at the head. Behind him were his three colleagues. Behind them was Glamug, shaking his baton or the pebbles in a gourd at the end of a stick. Then Thammash the chief and Angrogrim the greatest warrior. And then Wazwim, the singer, who was in one sense as much a witch doctor as Glamug, since most songs were sung for magical purposes. After Wazwim was Shivkaet, the carver and the painter, who did much of his work under the supervision of Glamug. His products were mostly used for magical purposes, too. Then came Dubhab, who had lost his smile and seemed much withdrawn and grouchy. After him came other males according to their unstated but well-recognized rank in their society. And then the women and children according to their ranks.

The flanks and the rear were guarded by the lesser warriors and juveniles who had not been "blooded" as yet. The "blooding," in most cases, would consist of a symbolic conflict during a ceremony. There was very little actual fighting between tribes. The hostilities with the Wotagrub had taken more casualties in a few minutes than even the oldest man, Kwakamg, remembered having taken place in his whole life. Occasionally a lone hunter or perhaps a couple of hunters had accidentally run into alien hunters and there had been some exchange of spears or rocks. And now and then a man had been killed or a woman or child ambushed. But these incidents were infrequent.

In fact, several days later, while Kwakamg was recounting the largest battle he remembered, which had taken place during the Winter of the Red Snow, Kwakamg dropped dead. Whether it was the excitement of the memory coupled with an age-weakened heart, or whether his heart would have given way at that moment anyway, no one knew. Gribardsun dissected him because he was eager to get data on the incidence of heart disease among the Magdalenians. Kwakamg was white-haired and wrinkled and had had a slight palsy. But the dissection convinced Gribardsun that Kwakamg was probably not more than sixty. His heart was that of an eighty-year-old man. At some time in Kwakamg's life he had had rheumatic fever. He had also had rheumatism, smallpox, and had lost about twelve teeth. But six had been knocked out during an encounter with a cave bear. The others had been rotten, and Glamug had pulled them out without much trouble for himself and only great pain for Kwakamg.

Two days later, Gribardsun delivered the baby of Meena, a sixteen-year-old woman, wife of Shimkoobt. Both the mother and baby would have died if Gribardsun had not been there, since he was forced to take the infant by caesarian.

Glamug told him that caesarians were not unknown. But almost always the mother died and the baby was lucky to survive.

Gribardsun recorded this data. And he wondered when the first caesarian had been performed. No one would probably ever know, since no time machine could yet go deeper into the past.

"So you have affected the future materially," Rachel said. "Who knows? If it weren't for you, many of us twenty-first centurians wouldn't exist. Perhaps even you wouldn't exist."

"Speculation is interesting but essentially useless," the Englishman said. "I have changed nothing. Before I was born, everything I had done in the past had been done."

"Let's not get involved in any more of these time paradoxes," Rachel said. "I always end up with a dizzy feeling, and slight sickness at the stomach, after trying to untangle the metaphysics and supermechanics of Time!"

"Time is something man will never comprehend," Gribardsun said. "Partly because Time is outside man. Man is, of course, partly *in* Time, but there are elements of Time that are completely exterior to him. He can't even see those elements and never will because they can't be put under the microscope or telescope or be detected by radiation-sensitive equipment."

He and Rachel were walking down the slope of a valley. He had three hares on a rope slung over his shoulder. The beasts had been caught in traps, and the two were headed for another trap they had set two days before. The snow covered the ground by about two feet. Tall green snow-laden firs and pines rose on every side, but presently they came to a clear stretch. A dozen or so large boulders were scattered around the clearing. Their breaths steamed, and above them a large eagle swung, running its stiff-winged shadow ahead of them.

Gribardsun had not wished to be alone with Rachel,

but she had asked if she could accompany him. He disliked saying no, because she had behaved toward him for months as if he were just another scientist. Apparently she and Drummond were now living with no more than the friction most married couples experienced.

"The thing to do is to enjoy Time as much as you can," he said. "Live as the beasts do. From day to day. If you think of the end of Time, that is, of your own death, accept it as part of Time. You can do nothing about it, so why worry about it?"

"But you, you're the exception—" Rachel said, and then she stopped. Her eyes were wide and her mouth open. Her hand was at her throat, as if she would choke off her words.

"I am?" he said. "Why?"

"I mean," Rachel said, "that you, or anybody, might be the exception. That's what I meant. What if somebody found a means to extend his life span for a very long time, and then . . . ?"

"And then what?" Gribardsun said. He had stopped and was looking down at her with large and bright gray eyes.

Rachel shivered, and yet she could not have been cold. The sun was warm and she was covered and hooded with the thin but very warm thermicron material.

"I was just speculating," she said. "Surely, sometime in man's history, somebody must have stumbled across an elixir of a sort, something which kept a man young for a very long time. Don't you think that's possible?"

"It's possible," he said, smiling. She shivered again.

"When I was a young man, I heard stories among the natives of Africa about witch doctors who had invented an elixir of youth. It was also supposed to confer immunity to all diseases. But mankind wishes for such an elixir and so he makes up stories to the effect that such a thing does exist."

"Well," Rachel said, "just suppose such a person as I postulated did exist? Wouldn't you think he'd become very lonely? He'd see those he loved get old and ugly and die. And his own sons, and his grandsons, would age and die. And he'd be bound to fall in love many times, and raise children, and each time his wife would inevitably die."

She stopped, licked her lips, and moved closer to him. Her chin was lifted high so she could look up into his eyes.

"Unless," she said, "this man knew how to make the elixir. Then he could keep his wife and his children young also. Of course, he'd have to swear them to secrecy, and that might be such a dangerous thing that he would hesitate. It would be difficult for most people to keep such a secret to themselves. Most people, I say."

"But not for you?" he said, smiling.

"Yes, but not for me!" she said.

"I hope you find someone who has the elixir," he said. "If he should exist. Which he won't in this era, of course. Although you never know. Perhaps some plant exists which could provide the basis of an elixir. And then that plant will become extinct. But the elixir only has to be used once. The effect of the elixir might be permanent, relatively speaking."

"Maybe I shouldn't be saying anything," she said. "But when you were gone, visiting the Wotagrub, Drummond and Robert and I had a long talk about you. We concluded that there was something very strange about your being chosen as a member of this expedition. And we agreed that there was something strange about your background. Every once in a while you let slip some peculiar remarks that can only be accounted for by your having lived a long long time, far longer . . . "

Gribardsun had not lost his smile. He said, "I wonder if your displacement in time hasn't resulted in some sort of shock. Shall we call it temporal shock? Or the temporal syndrome? A human being can't be catapulted backward in time, to an age so alien in nature, so savage, and so very far away from his own world, without suffering a neurosis or perhaps even psychosis."

"If that were true, then you'd be just as much in shock as we," she said. "But you're getting me off the track. I was . . . "

She stopped. He had looked up over her shoulder at something far up the hill. He had stiffened.

"What's wrong?" she said. She turned around and looked up the steep slope. But she could see only the sun-bright snow and the green and white firs and pines, the eagle; and several gray shadowy shapes—wolves—far to the right near the top of a ridge. But he was looking to the left.

"I thought I saw something moving up there," he said. "Among the trees."

She moved against him and put her arms around him without thinking about it. It was the expression of her long-repressed desire, and he knew it at once. She realized it several seconds later, but by then it was too late. She did not withdraw; she stood on her toes and kissed him.

The bullet tore the fabric of their solitude within an inch of their ears—or so it seemed—and then the report of the rifle reached them.

Gribardsun shoved her sprawling into the snow and dived after her.

Rachel had uttered a muffled scream. Now she raised her head, looking like a snow maiden. The powdery stuff was over her face and ringing her large blue eyes.

"It's Drummond!" she said. "But why would he do it? How could he? It's not like him! He's not violent! He's not a murderer!"

Gribardsun may have considered that her husband was the most probable suspect. But he said, "Let's not accuse anybody until we know for certain who . . ."

Another bullet cut off his speech; it came so close that it almost seemed to have severed the words issuing from his mouth. It threw up a spray of snow only an inch before him.

Gribardsun rolled to one side and then said, "Very good shooting, or the man's very lucky. He couldn't have seen me behind the snow, I don't think. Get over behind that boulder!"

Rachel crawled swiftly to the designated rock, and another bullet threw up snow a few inches from her foot. Gribardsun said, a moment later, "I think he's about four hundred yards away, judging from the difference in time between the bullet striking and the time it takes the report to reach us."

Rachel moaned. "What reason could Drummond have? We've never done anything!"

"Reason?" Gribardsun said. He did not add anything, but she understood him. Human beings were far more motivated by irrationalities than by reason.

Gribardsun waited until another bullet had gone by and then rolled over to the boulder behind which Rachel crouched. He broke open his .365 rifle to make sure that the barrel was unclogged by snow, and then he told Rachel to stay where she was.

He jumped up and dived into the snow, rolled, and was behind a tree.

Rachel heard two more shots and then could not resist looking around the side of the boulder. She could see neither man. The top of the hill looked empty of life. Gribardsun must be fairly near, but he was behind a tree somewhere up the hill.

She waited for an hour by her watch. Only one more shot was fired during that time. She cried and wiped the tears away and then cried some more. She could not believe that her husband was really trying to kill her. Perhaps he had been shooting just at Gribardsun, but no, those first bullets had come too near her as well. He must not have cared whether he struck her or Gribardsun.

Presently she heard John's voice far away. Cautiously, she looked over the boulder. He was a tiny figure near the top of the mountain. He was waving at her to come up. A moment later he used his amplifier. His voice bellowed down at her, like God's telling His worshipper to ascend the Mount of Judgment.

It took her half an hour to get to him. The snow was deep most of the way, and the slope was steep. By the time she reached him, she was breathing as if she had asthma.

She did not want to see what he was pointing at, but she knew that she must sooner or later. And she was also aware that she did not want to show weakness before John. She dreaded his contempt, even though she had never experienced it.

Drummond was sitting in a hollow of snow. His face was between his mittened hands, and he was rocking back and forth. His hood was off, permitting her to see a bloody patch on the back of his head. His rifle was gone.

Gribardsun pointed at tracks leading away from the hollow and down over the other side of the ridge.

"Drummond was watching us," he said. "But he claims that he did not shoot at us, and I believe him. Someone came up behind him while he was spying on us, hit him over the head, shot at us with his rifle, and then left with it before I could get close to him."

"It couldn't be Robert!" she said.

"I doubt it very much," John Gribardsun said. "But if it was an aborigine, he'd have to be one of our tribesmen, since nobody else would have the faintest notion how to operate a rifle. The only one who's had any practice at all is Dubhab, and he's not had enough to be as good a shot as the man who was shooting at us."

"Maybe—" Rachel said, and she stopped.

Drummond looked up from between his mittens at her. His eyes were large, bloodshot, and miserable.

"Maybe Drummond was shooting at us, and then the intruder knocked him over the head and took his rifle away," Gribardsun finished for her.

"That's a lie!" Drummond said.

"It's only a speculation," Gribardsun said. "And don't imply I'm a liar any more. You're in no position to be calling names or accusing anybody of anything."

"Are you all right, Drummond?" Rachel said. She sounded sympathetic, but she did not make any move toward him.

"My head feels as if I have a fracture."

Gribardsun examined his scalp and then applied the sonic photo camera to the wound. Six seconds later, the film slid out of the tiny box. He looked at it through a magnifying glass and said, "There's no fracture of the skull. But you do have a slight concussion."

"Slight!" Drummond said.

"You're lucky to be alive," Gribardsun said. "You escaped killing twice."

"Why don't you put me out of my misery?" Drummond said.

"Don't be an ass," the Englishman said, and he

lifted Drummond to his feet. "You saw us kissing, no doubt. That was entirely unpremeditated; it was brought about because of a peculiar concatenation of circumstances. Not that it might not happen again, if you continue to be such an utter nincompoop."

"A what?" Drummond said.

"An archaic word," Gribardsun said. "Another nail in the coffin of your absurd suspicions. You forget that I'm more than a doctor and a physical anthropologist. I'm also a linguist."

He turned Drummond over to Rachel, and she half supported him while Gribardsun led the way down the other side of the mountain. He followed the deep tracks of the intruder. Occasionally he halted and warned the others to get down in the snow while he reconnoitered. When the possibility of an ambush was cleared away, he motioned them to continue.

The tracks suddenly disappeared when they were within a quarter of a mile of the campsite. The man had taken to a pile of boulders and smaller rocks, the tops of which had been swept clean of snow by the wind. He had leaped from one bare spot to another. Since the rocks were widespread, and since there were many tracks from the tribespeople around the rocks, the man had effectively eluded them.

He would, however, have had to conceal the rifle and the box of ammunition he had stolen. This he could easily do by taking the rifle apart and concealing it under the heavy fur garments. But if he thought to hide it in his tent, he would soon be found out. There was very little privacy inside the camp and few places to hide anything inside a tent. He would have to conceal the rifle inside furs, and the first time one of his family bumped into the bundle, the contents would be detected. It was probable that the rifle and ammunition had been hidden somewhere in the several acres of rock detritus near the camp.

Gribardsun put Drummond inside his plastic hut and made another examination. Then he went straight to the tent of Dubhab. Leminak greeted him with her usual joy and unconcealed worship. Gribardsun gave no evidence that he was looking for her father. He chatted with her for a few minutes, then said that he mustn't be holding up her work, which was sewing a parka. Where was her father?

Laminak said that he was out hunting of course. She hoped he would bring home at least as much as Gribardsun had, she said, looking at the hares still slung over his shoulder.

Gribardsun saw nothing in her demeanor to indicate she was lying. Besides, he did not think that she would make the slightest effort to deceive him. She loved him more than anybody, even her father.

Gribardsun gave her a hare and left, though she was trying desperately to keep him by asking a string of questions. He said he would speak to her later, then stooped and went out through the exit. At that moment Dubhab left the woods nearby and approached the camp under the overhang of rock. He saw Gribardsun waiting for him but did not check his pace. He smiled when he got closer and loudly greeted him.

Gribardsun had decided by then that Dubhab had hidden the rifle—if he was the thief—and that it would be better not to let him know he was a suspect. He talked with him for a few minutes, inquired about his hunting, and was told that Dubhab had been very unlucky. Gribardsun mentioned that he had left a hare for his family, and walked away.

That evening, after everybody had eaten, he announced at the council fire that they would be moving on the next day. And their journey for many days would be hard. He wanted to get as far south as possible. Once they had reached a warmer land, they would stop.

The next day, he watched Dubhab as closely as possible. But the man went about his normal business in a normal manner.

Chapter 5

Drummond came out of his white cone several hours after dawn. He moved slowly as if he had aged considerably overnight or was in great pain. He reported only a slight headache, however. Again, he asserted that he was innocent.

"Rachel and I have had our trouble, no denying that," he said. "And she is very much attracted to you. I don't know whether it's because she is on the bounce from me or if she would have fallen for you in any event. Even I can see what she means by your animal magnetism. And you've become doubly attractive in this world; you could well have been born in it, you fit in with is so well.

"And I don't deny I've been jealous. But, damn it, I'm not a murderer! I'm a scientist! I didn't get my doctorate by lacking severe self-discipline. I have a tremendous amount of self-control. Too much, in fact. It's not my nature to kill, and even if it were, I have the strength to repress such an urge."

Gribardsun waited until he was through. He said, "All this talk means nothing. When I catch the man who took your rifle, I'll get his story from him, one way or another. Until then, let's drop the subject."

"But I don't want you suspecting me!" Drummond said. "You'll never trust me behind you again!"

"I don't trust anyone behind me," Gribardsun said. "Everyone is automatically suspect."

He walked away. An hour later the tribe was ready, and it started down the mountains toward the great plains of Spain. These were not the semideserts that Gribardsun had known. They were well watered and covered with grass and there were many trees. They also had an abundance of animal life: great herds of bison, horses; the giant aurochs and the infrequent mammoths and rhinoceroses. The lions of the plains were smaller than the cave lions; they resembled the African lion of the reservations of the twenty-first century.

Gribardsun said that even now he found it strange to see lions in snow. But then that was just because he had associated the big cats with the tropics. After all, the Siberian tiger and the snow leopard of the twentieth century (both extinct in the twenty-first) had lived quite well in freezing climates.

He decided to camp for several weeks. The place chosen would be, in approximately 11,000 years or so, the city of Madrid. He ignored the protests of the tribesmen, who said that he was contradicting himself in stopping here when he had said that they would not pause until they reached a warm country. He told them that he wanted to study the hunting habits of lions in snow and ice. Moreover, there was a tribe about six miles away which could provide another language for von Billmann's recorders.

Lramg'bud, a juvenile, was blooded at this time. With an atlatl and two spears, a stone axe and a knife, he went after a male lion that was eating a freshly killed horse. The lion acted as if it could not believe the stupidity of the man. Surely no one would be unintelligent enough to attack it while it was dining. But Lramg'bud went on in, looking brave enough, though there was no telling what his feelings were. The lion at last decided that he would not put up with the fool dancing around and stabbing at him. He charged, and the youth slammed a spear through the big cat's shoulder with an atlatl. The lion got up on three legs, and Lramg'bud drove his second spear deep into its chest. Despite this, the lion got to him and knocked his axe away with a bat of his massive paw. Lramg'bud seized the spear sticking from the chest and clung to it while the lion carried him backward. Suddenly, the beast collapsed; blood poured from its mouth; its eyes glazed. And Lramg'bud had a lion's head and lion's skin cloak to wear.

Everybody was happy, and the warriors feasted on lion meat that evening. Gribardsun ate his share raw. Lately he seldom ate cooked meat. Von Billmann had joked about this, and the Englishman had replied that he had always preferred raw meat. Von Billmann said that it was dangerous; raw meat was too likely to be infested with parasites. Gribardsun had merely smiled and continued chewing.

"It's not a question of when in Rome, do as the Romans do," Rachel said. "Even these savages cook their meat thoroughly. It disturbs them that you eat yours bloody."

"Chacun à son goût," Gribardsun said and licked the blood off the corners of his mouth. The fire lit his rugged and handsome face and seemed to be reflected in his gray eyes. Rachel turned away and went back to the women's feast. She had come over to the chief's "table" to ask him a question and had been unable to resist joining the conversation.

Drummond looked at Gribardsun with an indecipherable expression. When he saw the Englishman's eyes on him, he looked down. But he was doing only what everybody did who tried to outstare Gribardsun.

Three days later, they packed and left. Efforts to make friendly contact with the nearest strangers had failed. The tribe had picked up and decamped northward.

The fourth night after leaving the site of Madrid-to-be, somebody shot out the lock of the door of Gribardsun and von Billmann's hut, stuck the barrel in, and blazed away. After discharging five cartridges, the rifle was withdrawn, and the man who had fired ran away.

If the rifleman had moved the barrel around a wider arc, he would have struck both occupants a number of times. In which case it is doubtful that either would have lived, since the impact of the high-velocity and heavy bullets was deadly.

But he had made the mistake of blowing out the lock when he could instead have fired straight through one of the walls. And he had moved the muzzle only a few inches to either side, not enough to send the bullets past one of the small boulders set inside the hut to hold it down. They had simply ricocheted off the boulder and out again through the walls.

Though unhurt, the two men had been deafened by the explosions. They sat in their original positions for twenty or so seconds after the explosions ceased, unable to hear the slapping of the would-be killer's soft leather boots on the rock. Then Gribardsun, rifle in one hand, burst through the doorway, banging the door to one side and tearing it off with the impact of his body.

By then the camp was awake. Several torches were thrust into the embers of fires, and the people came out of their tents.

Gribardsun immediately ordered a head count.

Thammash and Glamug lined everybody up and had them call out by name.

Before the counting was done, a rifle exploded somewhere in the darkness. A bullet skimmed Gribardsun's shoulder. He rolled away into the darkness, out of the light of the torches, and then was up and into the nearby woods.

The Englishman had had many years of experience as a woodsman. He could move through the forest, winter or summer, without making a sound. But the man he was hunting had been born in a world where a man has to be one with the woods or starve. He had disappeared somewhere deep into the trees. Gribardsun finally found his tracks and started after him, avoiding but staying closely parallel to the tracks. Snow began to fall, and he realized that his quarry's trail would soon be covered. Moreover, if he did not return to the camp, he might find himself lost or bogged down.

The wind had come up, and the snow was pelting down when he got back to camp. By then, von Billmann had started the head count again. Gribardsun waited to one side grimly. He looked for Dubhab and did not see him and then, suddenly, Dubhab was coming out of his tent. He had gone back into it when the shot came from the woods, he said.

Nobody was missing. The rifleman had circled back and sneaked into camp during the hullabaloo.

The Englishman regarded him for a moment and then he, too, smiled.

"Light some more torches!" he said. "Robert, set up some lights and equipment in our hut! We'll give them the paraffin test!"

Von Billmann and the Silversteins looked puzzled.

Gribardsun spoke in Wota'shaimg so that the tribe could understand what he intended to do. He explained that when a man fired a rifle, he got some small particles of the gunpowder on his hand or on his clothes. This could be detected through the use of a substance known as paraffin. It would be easy to find out who had fired the rifle by examining the hands, or the gloves, of every man in the camp except, of course, those whom Gribardsun knew were not in the woods.

Von Billmann said in English, "I never heard of that test, John. Is that some more of your old lore?"

"The paraffin test was used at one time, Robert," Gribardsun said. "But it wasn't used exactly as I said. Nor could we use it under these conditions, even if we had the paraffin.

"That doesn't matter. What does is that the would-be killer will believe that we can detect him with these means, and he . . ."

Dubhab had suddenly started running. He went past Glamug and Thammash and Angrogrim, his short legs pumping rapidly, his face a twist of despair.

Gribardsun's hand moved; suddenly it held a steel knife. He threw it, it glittered in the torchlight, and then its hilt was sticking out of the bear fur over Dubhab's back.

Later, Gribardsun said that he believed in swift justice. He did not want a trial because that would have been too painful for Dubhab's family and there was no reason to make the man himself suffer. Moreover, if he had tried to capture the man, and had failed Dubhab might have gotten to his hidden rifle in time to use it.

The other scientists were shocked, though not as much as they would have been had they not had time to get used to this world. Justice in their world was often agonizingly slow. Everything that could be done to safeguard the rights of the accused and of the accuser was done. Moreover, no person had been executed for a crime for sixty years anywhere in the world. And prison was unknown except as a means for restraining dangerous people while they underwent therapy.

Gribardsun said, "I don't believe that we'll ever find the rifle."

Rachel cried, "Is that all you can think about? My God, you just killed him as if he were an animal! He didn't have his chance in a trial; you judged and convicted and executed him in two seconds!"

Gribardsun did not reply. He withdrew his knife and wiped it clean and then walked over to Thammash and Glamug and spoke briefly to them. Angrogrim picked up Dubhab and carried him to his tent, where he stretched him out a few feet in front of the entrance. Amaga, Abinal, Laminak and Neliska stared for a while, pale and tearless, at the body and then they went inside the tent and closed the flap.

By morning, Dubhab's body was frozen stiff. The funeral took all day, and he was buried under a pile of rocks in the midst of general mourning. That he had been a criminal and a traitor did not matter after he had died. He was then one of the tribe and to be treated with all the honors of any brave warrior and good hunter, which he had been most of his life.

Afterward, Gribardsun found what obligations he had taken upon himself by killing Dubhab. He was now responsible for Dubhab's family. It was up to him to provide for them.

Abinal's attitude toward the Englishman did not seem to have changed. But when he became a man, he would have to decide whether to forgive Gribardsun or kill him. He knew that; everybody knew that. For the time being, the matter would be put into abeyance.

Amaga did not care who took care of her. Gribardsun told her that he would protect her and hunt meat for her. But he was not her mate and did not intend to be.

Amaga was indignant and justly so, since tribal custom decreed that Gribardsun should replace Dubhab in all his duties. He stated simply that he did not care to. Amaga then told all the tribe, but for the first time the tribe did not dare to punish a custom breaker.

The woman sullenly accepted the reality of the situation, but a short time later she brightened. Perhaps Gribardsun preferred the beautiful and hard-working Neliska as his mate?

Gribardsun said he was considering that.

Rachel looked shocked.

Drummond smiled but did not say anything to her.

Neliska looked happy.

Laminak, weeping, ran away.

Rachel said, "But you'll be leaving in a few years! Would you just walk out on her? Or were you thinking of taking her back with you as a specimen? That would be cruel; she could never adjust to the bewildering modern world. Anyway, she's a tribal creature, and she'd die if she were cut off from her people."

"I said I was considering her as a mate," Gribardsun said. "I didn't say when I would come to a decision. I rather believe that by the time I'd be able to speak for her, she would be long married."

Rachel later said to Drummond, "I don't think I'll ever understand that man. His thought processes are too deep. Or maybe just too different. There's something not quite—normal?—human, about him."

"Time keeps a man human. But eternity would give him a nonhuman dimension," Drummond said. "Perhaps he isn't quite human. But I just can't go along with your theories about someone finding the elixir. I just can't believe in such a phenomenon as an elixir. Especially in the nineteenth century, which would be when Gribardsun was born, if you were right. That business about the first time machines and the limits of the 1870's indicates that something is rotten."

At the time this conversation took place, they had just crossed the half-frozen Guadiana River. Four days later, after they had established a camp on the south side of a heavy brake of trees, Drummond attacked Gribardsun.

The assault was entirely verbal, although there was one moment when the tall thin physicist seemed on the point of attacking the Englishmen with his fists.

Ever since the incident of the stolen rifle, Gribardsun had refused to let Drummond hunt with him. He went either with Rachel or von Billmann, and Drummond found that a tribesman was always shadowing him when Gribardsun was out on a hunt. He said nothing about this, not even to his wife, until the evening of the fourth day after crossing the Guadiana. Gribardsun said that they would camp there for several days while he went out hunting wild horses with a dozen tribesmen. He intended to restrict himself this time to native weapons again. Von Billman would go along as "shotgun," as usual.

Drummond belligerently said that he intended to accompany them.

"Fine," Gribardsun said. "If you leave your firearms here."

"Why should I?" Drummond leaped up, his hands balled.

"I want to make sure there are no accidents."

"Accidents, hell! You mean you want to make sure I don't shoot you in the back, is that it?" Drummond yelled.

"That is exactly it," Gribardsun said coolly.

"Damn you, you have no right to suspect me of trying to kill you!" Drummond screamed. "I admit I was watching you two, and I have every right to do so, and from what I saw, my suspicions were justified! But I did not shoot at you! It was Dubhab, and you *know* it!"

"I don't know any such thing," Gribardsun said. "As for your suspicions being valid, what did you see? Nothing really, because nothing happened. Nor will it, unless you bring it about with your psychotic jealousy. Frankly, Silverstein, I don't understand what's happened to you. I saw your psych ratings, and they indicated a stable character and a reasonably well-adjusted marriage. But all of a sudden you go ape."

Gribardsun smiled when he said the last two words, and Drummond wondered why, but he did not ask.

"I think that the sudden thrust into a strange world, the temporal dislocation, caused an emotional imbalance. Let's hope that you regain your normal state of emotion before long. Otherwise, you may end up insane or dead."

"Is that a threat?" Drummond shouted.

"I don't make veiled threats. I am merely stating likely alternatives."

Gribardsun paused and then said, "I am sorry that this happened, because an efficient scientific team needs as little friction and as much good will as possible among its members. We have a relatively short time to do much, and we shouldn't be wasting it with human pettiness. So . . ."

"Pettiness!" Drummond yelled. "You call losing my wife a pettiness? Being accused of attempted murder is a pettiness?"

"You haven't lost your wife nor have Rachel and I done anything to deserve your condemnation. Nor have I accused you of attempted murder. But you are definitely under suspicion."

Drummond lifted his open hands to the night sky

and said, "How long? How long? Do I have to go the rest of my life under suspicion? What charges will you bring when we get back? Would you wreck my career on the basis of nothing at all, circumstantial evidence and weak at that? What can I do to clear myself? Would you hold a trial?"

"There is no way of clearing you," Gribardsun said. "So I propose that we continued to work together and try to get along together as best we can. I just do not propose to put myself in a position where I will be at your mercy."

"Look at her! Look at her!" Drummond said, pointing at Rachel. "The devoted wife! The trusting spouse! My beautiful innocent loving Rachel! She believes *you!* She thinks I *was* trying to shoot you!"

"Or her. Or both of us," Gribardsun said.

"Drummond, you're sick," Rachel said. "I just can't believe that you would try to kill anybody. I've known you too long. And yet, I never knew you to be jealous, at least, not abnormally so. Something has happened to you, and it makes me sick, just simply sick in the pit of my soul. But . . ."

"Go to hell! Go to hell, both of you!" Drummond said. He looked at von Billmann, who had been sitting with head bowed, sipping on his coffee.

"You can go to hell too!"

'What did I do to you?" von Billmann said.

"You believe *them,* not *me!*" Drummond said, and stamped off into the darkness.

The others were silent. They had been sitting on inflatable cushions around a wood fire. Their huts were two white cones in the firelight. From thirty yards away came the sound of many voices as the tribesmen called back and forth and laughed at jokes. They were happy. Nobody was sick, and they had plenty of meat.

The explorers had made their camp some distance

from the others because they had wanted to discuss their plans for tomorrow without interruption. They intended to study the region for three days before moving on. But Drummond's outbursts had cut off the planned conversation.

Rachel looked out into the starless and moonless night and said, "I hope he comes back soon. It's dangerous wandering around out there. He's only got his pistol, too."

"I'd suggest a physical and mental examination for him," Gribardsun said. "But he would object, and he might be justified. I don't know how objective I myself could be in my examination."

"Do you suppose it could be temporal shock?" Rachel said.

"I think so," von Billmann said. "I'm only just now getting my sense of reality back. For a long time everything seemed distorted, out of focus slightly, you might say. Weird. Simply not true to reality. How about you, John? Did you feel anything like that?"

"The first three or four days," Gribardsun said. "Though even that was not an overpowering feeling by any means."

Von Billmann went to bed. The tribesmen crawled into their tents and tied the flaps shut. Rachel and Gribardsun sat before the fire and stared into its flames or looked now and then into the snow-white night. The only sound was the crackling of the firewood, the distant howl of a wolf, and an even more distant bellowing from some aurochs in some snow-walled area.

After a while, Rachel looked up across the fire at Gribardsun. Tears were running down her cheeks.

"Drummond and I should be so happy," she said. "We don't really have any reasons for friction between us. We share so many common interests, and before he got moody he was sometimes amusing, though too serious most of the time. But not always. And we were chosen to go on this expedition, and that alone should have kept him happy. But . . ."

She wiped the tears away and swallowed and then said, "But something happened. He's so miserable and unhappy. And everything is just ruined for us, just ruined. It'll never be like it was. It just can't be. And if he keeps on the way he has, he'll end up trying to kill you or me or both. Or probably he'll kill himself. He has a tendency to turn his anger inward against himself."

Gribardsun said, "Most human beings seem to go wrong in one way or another to a greater or lesser degree. They're much less stable than animals, and this instability is the price humans pay for their sentience and their complicated emotional system. Self-consciousness and the power of speech are the requisites, though not the only ones, for progress in man. But man pays for his greater potentiality by a greater vulnerability to imbalance. And your Drummond is just one of the ten billion imbalances of the twenty-first century."

"And that theory makes me one of the ten billion unbalanced too, right?" she said. "Well, God knows that I know that. But what about you, John?"

"Human, all too human," he said, smiling slightly. "But my early life, the really formative period, was rather peculiar. I'm not sure that I look at the world through an entirely human prism. But that doesn't really make much difference in my response to the world. The kind of imbalance that I am talking about is largely genetic. The very nature of a man's nervous system forces him to stumble; he makes mistakes and errors and reacts in a unique egotistic manner to the world, and he gets sick. Mental sickness is the sentient's way of life, you might say.

"I suppose I was lucky. I have an unusual stability. But for that I must pay a price, of course. What that price is . . ."

"Oh, you're so mysterious!" she said. "You've been talking a lot and you've said almost nothing meaningful! What is all this about your early years? Weren't you raised by human beings? Surely you aren't some sort of Mowgli or Romulus or Remus? Everybody would have heard about it if you had been, and, besides, the very idea is ridiculous. And I happen to know that you were born on the Inner Kenyan Reservation and you were raised by your parents and the black natives."

"That's what the records say."

"I know what you've been doing with all this mysterious nonsensical talk. You've been taking my mind off Drummond! You're very clever. But thoughtful. I thank you for your concern. But I have to worry about him. What is he doing out there, wandering in the snow? He might get lost or some bear or lion might get him, or . . ."

"This isn't mountain country so there aren't any bears, and besides, the bears are hibernating," he said. "And we haven't seen a lion for days."

"The wolves!" she said.

"When he left he knew what he was walking into," Gribardsun said. "I suggest that you go to bed and put him out of your mind, if you can. He'll be coming home soon enough, and in the morning we'll see how he feels. We do have work to do, you know, and . . ."

He started to rise, but she said, "Sit down, John. Please! Just for a moment! Don't leave me!"

He lowered himself on the cushion again and said, "Very well. I'll stay a little while, if it will help you."

She leaned forward and said, "John! Do you or do you not love me?"

He smiled slightly again, and she said, "Don't laugh at me!"

"I wouldn't do that," he said. "I was just thinking of —well, never mind. There were women bold enough even in my youth. I knew more than one who would come out with the same question if she felt the need for an answer. But I sometimes forget how free modern women are. That, however, is neither here nor there, is it? You asked, and you shall receive.

"I find you very attractive, Rachel, and if you were free, I might ask you to marry me. But you aren't free, and I am old-fashioned. I don't believe in adultery, and I wouldn't try to break up a marriage or take advantage of the fact that it's breaking up. I don't love you with the intensity or the passion you meant when you asked me if I loved you. I do like you very much. But I don't love you."

There was a silence. Something white, a huge bird, glided past the snow-laden branches of the trees just on the edge of the firelight.

Finally, Rachel said, "I thought you weren't in love with me, but I was hoping that you were and that you felt you couldn't say or do anything because I was still married. But you don't love me, and I thank you for telling me so honestly, even though it does hurt."

"I seldom have regrets," he said, "since regret changes nothing. But I am sorry that this whole affair developed. It's not only making you and Drummond unhappy, and making Robert miserable and myself uneasy; it's decreasing the scientific efficiency of all four of us."

"And we have an obligation to those who sent us here," she said. "I know. But what can I do to make things better?"

"Call me when Drummond gets in," he said. "I'll get

up, and we'll have this out before breakfast, if he shows up soon enough, of course."

"I don't know that he'll listen to reason any more."

"Then he won't, and we'll proceed from there."

"You're so practical," she said. "And so self-controlled."

"I've had much practice," he said. He rose and walked to his hut and then turned.

"I don't like to leave you alone, but there really is no point in staying up. If Drummond hasn't returned by morning, I may go out after him. He is an adult and so shouldn't have to be watched as if he were a child. But I am the head of this expedition, and it's up to me to keep watch on my people."

Rachel sat for ten minutes by the fire and then went into her hut.

Chapter 6

The first paleness of dawn acted as alarm clocks on the Wota'shaimg. The light seemed to penetrate the skins of their tents. The light touched their eyelids, and their lids opened. They crawled out of their tents into the start of a light snowfall. They went into the woods and emptied themselves, and then the women poked the embers buried under deep ashes and piled on wood shavings made by flint knives and then put on more wood. The fires were roofed and partially walled with boughs laid over each other in two layers. The snow was beginning to pile up on the fire huts, as they were called. The men gathered around the fire, hawking, blowing their noses, spitting and grumbling. They talked about the chances for hunting, which did not look good. Fortunately they had plenty of meat and the partially digested contents of bison and deer stomachs. The could afford to lie around the camp for a week, if they had to do so. By lying around they did not mean idleness. They would be repairing their spears and harpoons and working new flint and ivory and bone points, carving bone and ivory figurines of animals for use in magic, and figures of women to bring about increased fertility.

The three scientists ate their breakfast in a gloomy silence. Immediately afterward, Gribardsun said that he would go out and look for Drummond. The others volunteered to go with him, but he said that he could travel faster alone.

He put food, ammunition, and a small camera in his backpack and left. He carried collapsible snowshoes in the pack too, but would not use these until out of sight of the tribesmen. It was agreed that the explorers would not introduce any technological innovations to the Magdalenians. Snowshoes were, according to the twenty-first century anthropologists, not known to the Europe of 12,000 B.C. But the explorers used them only when they were unobserved by humans.

Gribardsun thought that this was an unnecessary precaution. Obviously, since late Paleolithic Europe had not known showshoes, then they would not be introduced by the time travelers. Thus, why worry? Use them in sight of the tribesmen. Teach the tribesmen how to make them. The knowledge would be lost because it had been lost.

However, the agreement had been made, so he would stick to it.

Once around a low hill and out of sight of the Wota'shaimg, he put on the snowshoes and set out swiftly on Drummond's trail. The physicist had gone around the hill and cut on a straight line across the plain, which was about two miles wide. He had not, as Gribardsun had suspected he would, hung around to spy on him and Rachel. Evidently he wanted to get as far away as possible.

As the Englishman pushed across the flat and comparatively treeless plain, the snow began to fall more heavily. Before he reached the low hills at the other end of the plain, the tracks were completely filled in.

Gribardsun stopped among the trees and considered.

He could keep on a straight line, hoping that Drummond had done the same. Or he could describe large circles, hoping to come across some sign of the man. Or he could do the sensible thing and return to camp. Let Silverstein, who had put himself in this mess, get himself out of it.

But Gribardsun's obligations included doing all he could to make the expedition a success. If he allowed Silverstein to die, he would be cheating the world of the physicist's labors. There was an immense amount of work for each member of the expedition and if one were eliminated, the others couldn't possibly replace him.

Besides, he just did not like the idea of letting the man wander around until he died even if it was his own fault. There was a time when he would not have cared if anyone lived or died unless the person's fate had happened to touch his own interests. But time had changed that.

He decided to take the straight line for another half a mile and then describe a spiral. He had traveled perhaps two miles and seen not a sign of Drummond when he heard faint sounds far to his right. He went through a pass between two low hills covered with firs. Beyond was a series of broad low hills which ran for half a mile. On the other side was a low mountain, and at the base of this were twelve men. They were on their bellies, working their way through the snow behind various large boulders. Their goal was Drummond Silverstein, half hidden behind a large boulder. He was firing about once a minute to drive the men back. But they were slowly decreasing the distance between them.

Gribardsun watched them for a while. They were big men with light brown or blond hair and light skins. They wore bear or bison skins; they carried spears, axes, and leather slings and stones. Two lay face down on the snow with small pools of frozen blood radiating out from them. They knew what the thunder stick could do and yet they were still going after the man using it. This required high courage or a low intelligence or possibly a combination of both.

Gribardsun walked out from behind the tree he had been using as a spy post and slogged through the snow toward the fight. A few seconds later he dived into the snow. A bullet had screamed by his head.

He did not cry out to Drummond that he had made a mistake. Drummond must have recognized him; the fact that he was carrying a rifle was enough to identify him. It was possible that Drummond was in a near mindless frenzy and was shooting at anything that moved. That often happened to men without experience when they were first in battle. However, he did not think that this was the situation. Drummond had certainly been cool and deliberate enough about firing at the natives with his revolver.

Gribardsun began to work his way to the left toward a stand of snow-laden trees part way up the hill. But the natives had seen him, and five of them were coming through the snow toward him. They were yelling and brandishing their spears in their gloved hands.

They certainly made excellent targets for Silverstein, but he did not fire at them. It was then that Gribardsun decided that Silverstein had shot at him knowing who he was. Now Silverstein was hoping that the natives would do what he had failed to do.

Gribardsun, still lying in the snow, raised his rifle, which was set for single-shot action, and fired over the heads of the men advancing upon him. He did not think that would stop them, but he would make the effort. After that, if they continued, they deserved what they got.

They kept advancing, though they sank into the snow to their knees.

Gribardsun fired with about twelve seconds between each shot. He wanted the survivors to appreciate the fact that no shot was now missing and that he was taking his time. But three fell before the two remaining decided to make off. They slogged away at right angles to their former path, determined to get away from both riflemen.

By then Silverstein had hit two more men in the snow, and the rest had decided that it would be best to retreat.

Gribardsun had quit firing, but Silverstein knocked over every man who stood up.

The total was fourteen dead. Somewhere nearby was a tribe which had lost much of its adult male population.

Gribardsun thought that Silverstein had truly gone insane.

By then he was behind a tree. He adjusted the bullhorn amplifier around his neck and roared, "Throw your gun out, and come out with your hands up!"

"So you can shoot me down in cold blood!" Drummond's amplifier thundered back.

"You know I wouldn't do that!" Gribardsun said. "You're a sick man, Drummond! You need medical care! That's all I'm concerned about! I want you to get well so you can do your work! We need you! And you need us!"

"I don't need you or anybody! I'm just going to keep on moving until I can go no more! And then I'll die!"

Gribardsun was silent for a while. The snow had ceased falling, and the grayness overhead was breaking up. Several times in the next ten minutes the sun shone through momentary brighter patches. It fell on the dark bodies scattered around the open arena. From downwind came the faraway cry of wolves. These may have smelled the blood and might be on their way to the promised feast. If so, they would be late, because six ravens had just flown in the alighted near a body. But there was enough to feed a hundred ravens.

The big black birds cautiously approached the body and then, deciding that it was not playing possum, tore at it. The eyes disappeared down black throats; the lips were pecked and stripped away; the tongue began to shred away in sharp beaks.

Gribardsun watched the eating indifferently. If anything, he approved. Ravens were one method for getting rid of garbage, of keeping the world clean.

But Silverstein could not stand the sight. He fired, and a raven flew apart in a spray of black feathers The others took off cawing and flew around describing black interrogation marks. When they fluttered back to the original corpse, they were scared away by another shot. This missed them but struck the head of the corpse and split it open. The ravens returned a second time and began to eat the blood and the brains. Silverstein did not shoot at them again.

Gribardsun stuck his head completely around the tree trunk, only to jerk it back. He was too late, of course, but the bullet gouged out a big piece of trunk and screamed off to the right. A few pieces of wood were stuck in the left side of his face. He picked them out while the blood froze on his cheek.

A few minutes later he jumped. Something had cracked loudly in the woods behind him.

It could have been the cold splitting open a branch, but he could not afford not to investigate. He crawled away, keeping the tree between himself and Silverstein until he got over a low ridge. His scouting revealed nothing except a fox which exploded from beneath a snow-heavy bush and, a minute later, the hare which the fox had been hunting.

Gribardsun watched the rodent with its big hairy feet bound along on top of the thin frozen crust of the snow. And then darkness exploded in him.

When he awoke, he had a sharp pain in the back of his head. He was lying on his side, and his hands were tied behind him. A pair of bison-hide boots were directly in front of his eyes. He looked up along wolf-hide trousers and a spotted black and white horse-hide parka. The man had a long dark beard with red undertones, thick black eyebrows and greenish eyes. He held a reindeer antler-tipped spear.

Gribardsun turned over slowly and saw six other strangers.

A moment later, three more came through the snow with a fourth whose hands were tied behind him.

"This is a fine mess you've gotten us into!" Drummond said.

Gribardsun might have smiled at this if his head had not hurt so much. A stone axe must have been thrown at him. That had to be so, since he was sure that not even an aboriginal woodsman could get close enough to hit him with a weapon in hand before he heard him.

He was sure that they had not arrived after the firing had ended. They must have been burrowed down in the snow, able to see him without his seeing them. Then, when he turned his back, one had gotten up slowly and thrown his axe.

He was surprised that he was still alive, but he was glad. While he lived, he had hope.

A big man lifted him up and set him on his feet. Then he knocked him down again with a fist in his solar plexus.

Gribardsun writhed around for a while, sucking in

air, though he was not as badly hurt as he pretended. He had had time to tense his muscles and also to throw himself slightly backward to ride with the blow.

The big man picked him up again, raised his fist, probably expecting Gribardsun to wince, and then lowered it at a word from a man who seemed to be the chief.

Gribardsun and Silverstein were led away to the south with a spearman behind each to prod him if he lagged. Their snowshoes had been left behind. Either the strangers had not see them use them, and so did not understand their use, or they were ignoring what they had seen because they did not fully comprehend it. But one man carried Drummond's revolver in his belt. The chief carried Gribardsun's rifle.

They had gone roughly half a mile when they saw a dozen or so gray shapes drift along the side of the hill, sliding in and out between the trees. The wolves were on their way to the feast.

After two miles of hard walking—or wading— through heavy snow that was sometimes waist-deep, they came to the camp. This was pitched against the south side of a steep hill and consisted of thirty-three wigwam-like tents. Trenches had been cut through the twenty-foot-high drifts to connect the tents. But snow was a good thermal insulation material, and as long as the tents did not collapse, they would keep the inhabitants warm. As Gribardsun was to find out, the tribesmen had dug out much of the snow immediately around the tents, leaving the top projections untouched. Thus, there was not as much weight on the tents as there seemed at first sight.

At the moment, Gribardsun was in no position to make detailed observations. Some of the women, on hearing of the disastrous casualties, launched screams and wails to the skies and their nails at the faces of the prisoners. Both men suffered deep gashes before the men pulled the women off. Gribardsun, however, kicked three women in the stomach, knocking out two and making the third vomit. He could have killed all three but thought he would be better off if he did not.

The big man who had hit him with his fist laughed when the women went sailing out of the pack. He slapped Gribardsun several times in the face after he rescued him, but not in a vengeful spirit. The man was grinning gap-toothed as he hit Gribardsun, as if he enjoyed seeing the women hurt. He also enjoyed hitting the prisoner, but he wasn't out to hurt him badly.

The prisoners were led through a trench of snow which rose high over Gribardsun's six-foot-three head. The central tent of the three concentric circles of tents was the largest. The chief lived in this with two adult women—his mother, apparently, and his wife—two juvenile females, a juvenile male, a six-year-old boy and a year-old girl. Wooden frames held the butchered carcasses of a deer and a quarter of a bison and other frames held spears and axes and cutting and chopping stones and sewing equipment of bone and sinew. A single fire in the center, confined in a stone hearth, sent blue smoke upward to the narrow opening in the top. It also sent much of the smoke around the tent.

The occupants were naked except for loin strips, though the temperature was about ten degrees above zero Fahrenheit except very near the fire. The tent stank of stale sweat, saliva burning in the fire, wet furs near the fire, rotting teeth, gummy dirt, rotten meat on some bones in a corner, and excrement in two open dug-out trunks of wood used as chamber pots.

After being out in the open, the stench was almost

as bad as a fist blow. But both men had encountered this every time they had entered a winter tent of the Wota'shaimg. Gribardsun had adapted—or at least had not complained—almost immediately. Silverstein had never really become at ease in the stench.

Three men pointed their spears at the two while the women removed the packs from their backs. All their clothes except their shorts were taken off. To get the parkas and undershirts off, their hands were untied. Gribardsun estimated his chances of breaking loose and decided against them. Even if he could get past the spears inside the tent, and the mob outside, he would be naked. He still might escape freezing if he ran all the way back to camp. He did not have these people's tolerance for cold, but he had more than most twenty-first centurians.

However, his chances at this time were just too slim. He would wait.

When his hands were retied, they were fastened in front of him. This was an advantage, but his ankle was tied by a tough sinew to the bottom of a tent pole. Silverstein was similarly tethered. The sinew was long enough for them to sit by the fire, which they did without objection from anyone. The chief and the big man seemed amused by the shivering of their prisoners.

"What do you think is going to happen to us?" Drummond said through chattering teeth.

"I don't know," Gribardsun said. "But since we killed so many, somewhere near half their adult males, we'll probably be required to suffer for it."

"Torture?"

"It's not outside the realm of possibility," Gribardsun said.

The men left. The prisoners were in the charge of the juvenile male and the women. The juvenile sat on a pile of furs and pointed a spear at them. The women sat or squatted near the edge of the tent and looked intently at their guests. One of the young females was quite pretty, if the dirtiness of her hair and face and the streak of mucus running from nose to lip were discounted. She looked back into Gribardsun's eyes for a long time before dropping her gaze. She wore only a strip of wolf fur around her waist, revealing a well-rounded and full-breasted form. Her face was a modified and attractive version of her father's. But her mother's sagging fat figure was a sad forecast.

Gribardsun was not that taken by her, but he did hope he could somehow use her to escape. So he gazed admiringly at her, smiled, and even winked once.

That was a mistake. She leaped up shrieking and plunged out through the opening.

A minute later, the angry voices of the chief and other men were at the entrance, and then the chief entered with a man whose painted face and one-eyed *baton de commandement* indicated the witch doctor. They were followed by the big man who had previously hit Gribardsun and several others. The juvenile male was standing up, his spear jabbing at Gribardsun. His skin was pale and his knees were shaking. The other women looked frightened. The juvenile was the only one who had seen the wink.

Gribardsun could understand nothing of the words shouted at him, of course. But he understood after several minutes of dancing and chanting by the doctor that he should not have winked. To this tribe, that was a form of the evil eye.

Gribardsun did not know what to do next. If he winked at the witch doctor, for instance, to show him that his magic was stronger, then the witch doctor might logically decide to put Gribardsun's eyes out.

What followed was unexpected but not unwelcome.

In this tribe, virtue, that is, white magic, that is, the tribe's own magic, triumphed over evil, that is, black magic, that is, the magic of another tribe.

But the magic must be put to the test, and so Gribardsun was taken outside where he and the big man entered a small arena dug out of the snow. Silverstein was taken along. The big man stripped naked, and Gribardsun's bonds were untied and his shorts removed. The adult males then crowded around the walls of the snow pit, and juvenile males and some of the other women pressed in behind them.

The big man was about six-foot-five and broader-shouldered, heavier-legged and thicker-armed than Gribardsun. He had some fat but not enough to give the impression of obesity.

Gribardsun understood without being told that this was to be trial by combat. He wondered, briefly, if this custom had actually arisen in this tribe and spread out from there. But he knew that it was doubtful that one small group would have originated the custom. In any event, no one would ever know, since study of this period was so restricted.

He hopped up and down and flexed his legs and arms and worked his fingers to restore his circulation. His shivering however, had stopped.

The big man, smiling confidently, walked up to Gribardsun with his arms out and his hands open.

Silverstein, shivering in one corner of the arena, guarded by the juvenile, expected Gribardsun to win. Though the tribesman was bigger, Gribardsun knew all the philosophies and techniques of twenty-first century schools of hand-to-hand fighting. He should be able to chop his opponent down with karate or judo in short order.

But the Englishman at first made no attempt to use anything but brute strength. He grabbed the tribesman's hands in his and waited. The big man, grinning, pushed against his smaller opponent. Gribardsun dug his naked heels into the snow and pushed back. The two slipped back and forth and then, suddenly, Gribardsun twisted the other man's hands, and the man dropped sideways onto the snow. The man struck heavily. The spectators grunted, or said something like, "Uhu-nga!"

His grin lost, the man got to his feet. Gribardsun seized his hands again and yanked downward and inward, and when the man was was near enough, brought up his knee and drove it against the chin beneath the thick beard.

This time the man had great difficulty getting to his feet.

Gribardsun helped him up, grabbed him by the back of the neck and his thigh and lifted him above his head. He turned around and around, slowly, smiling at the awed tribespeople, and then heaved the man, who must have weighed at least 280 pounds, over their heads and against the edge of the arena. The man struck it side-on, slid down, and lay at its bottom motionless.

The witch doctor advanced from the crowd, shaking his baton and muttering something rhythmic. He brought the end of the baton under Gribardsun's nose, held it there, and then moved it from side to side.

Gribardsun suddenly grabbed the baton, tore it from the doctor's grasp, and sent it spinning far out into the snow.

The doctor turned gray under the paint on his face and chest.

The next step was up to the tribesmen. Silverstein hoped they would not try something simple and logical, such as launching every spear they had against the two prisoners.

Nobody moved. Everybody stared at Gribardsun.

He smiled and walked toward the exit of the arena.

They gave way before him, and he took Silverstein's hand and led him back to the chief's lodge. There they sat down by the fire. Gribardsun added wood to it despite a muttered protest from the old woman who had not witnessed the combat outside.

The witch doctor and the chief entered. Gribardsun looked at the fire and ignored them. The doctor danced around the fire, passing behind Gribardsun and shaking his baton, which he had rescued, over the Englishman's head. He went around the fire widdershins twelve times and stopped on the other side of the fire just opposite Gribardsun. He raised the baton to his eye and looked through the hole in its end at Gribardsun.

Gribardsun raised his eyes and stared back at the doctor, then made an O with his thumb and first finger and stared at the doctor through that.

The witch doctor became pale.

"When among the Romans, out-Roman them," Gribardsun said to Silverstein.

He stood up and walked around the fire and seized the doctor by the nose and twisted it.

The doctor yelped with pain and flung his baton across the tent.

Gribardsun released the nose and went to the side of the tent and picked up the baton. It was of carved bone, and the hole in its end was large enough so that the shaft of a spear could be thrust through it. Originally, in the nineteenth century, the scientists had thought that the *batons de commandement* were for use in magical rites only. Then they had decided, in the twentieth century, that the batons were used to straighten out shafts. The truth, as the expedition had discovered, validated both theories. Some batons were used as physical tools and some as magical tools. In a sense, the magical batons were also shaft straighteners, since they were used by the witch doctors to straighten—or to bend—the invisible shafts that bound the universe together. The witch doctors kept the philosophy of the use of batons as a guild secret, transmitting the knowledge only to their successors. Gribardsun had tried to get Glamug to tell him the arcana of his trade, but Glamug had refused. However, by using a highly sensitive directional microphone, Gribardsun had eavesdropped on the school Glamug conducted for his two sons. He knew that the bone or wood or ivory baton was considered to be powerful. But a doctor who was powerful enough to use his own fingers to form the magical shaft-straightening hole was dreaded. There were very few. In fact, Glamug had never actually seen one. But the great doctor of tribal history—Simaumg—had used only his own fingers.

Gribardsun assumed that this tribe had its equivalent of Simaumg, and that its doctor would be aware of the dangerousness of such a man.

He was right. The witch doctor gave way completely. He lowered his baton and stared wide-eyed at Gribardsun. Then he reversed the baton and walked around the fire and handed it to him. The Englishman passed his finger through the hole in it several times and handed it back to the doctor.

Silverstein had watched all this bewildered. Gribardsun explained and then told him to put on his clothes. He doubted that anyone would interfere.

The chief and the witch doctor conferred in low tones for a while on the other side of the fire. Gribardsun got tired of waiting for them to come to a decision. He got up and put on his own clothes and resumed his place by the fire. Silverstein took out his pocket transceiver and soon got into contact with

Rachel. He described as best he could their situation and location.

"We were their prisoners, and I suppose we still are," Drummond said. "But, somehow, John has gotten the upper hand. I don't know how long he can keep it, though."

Silverstein confined himself to reporting the situation, though Rachel tried to get him to talk about his running away. Gribardsun gestured, and Silverstein brought the transceiver to him.

"Don't come after us," he said to Rachel. "You might upset the rather delicate balance of the situation. We'll keep in touch. I'll report in an hour."

"And if you don't?" Rachel asked.

"Then you can come after us. But if this tribe loses any more men, it's going to perish."

That evening the chief, the doctor, the big man (subdued and somewhat banged up), and a white-haired old man ate with the two prisoners in the tent. They tried to carry on a conversation with sign language. The chief managed to get across the idea that they were not prisoners but that the tribe could use the help of the two. By then the firearms had been returned to Gribardsun, who used signs to indicate that he would use his rifle to get meat for them.

Gribardsun also tried to find out from them what had happened to cause them to attack Silverstein, but he failed. Silverstein stuck to his story that they had jumped him, and he had been forced to shoot them. Gribardsun did not say anything about his narrow escape from one of Drummond's bullets. But he did not return the revolver to Drummond, nor did Drummond protest when Gribardsun dismantled the pistol and put the parts in his pack.

He did object when the Englishman said they

would spend the night in the tent and perhaps stay for several days.

"They'll murder us in our beds!" he said. "They must be just waiting to catch us off guard. My God, we killed almost half their men!"

"But through what is, to them, magical means," Gribardsun said. "So they expect us to reimburse them somehow. We are under obligation to them. At least, that is the feeling I get. And, in a way, we are obligated."

"But we can't support everybody we run across!" Silverstein protested. "You've already got Dubhab's family on your hands. In fact, the whole tribe, since they've come to depend more and more on you. Would you add another tribe to your entourage?"

"We are intruders," Gribardsun said. "Our presence is unnatural, if anything that exists in nature can be said to be unnatural. We are here to observe and study. But our very intrusion upsets the natural order of things, so that we are not observing things as they would be if we were not here. We constitute an example of Heisenberg's Principle of Uncertainty, but in a social sense. We can't but affect what we would like to see in its natural state. So our observations are necessarily distorted or qualified."

"I know that!" Silverstein said impatiently.

"Yes, but the point is that if we come to these people and bring catastrophe and ruin, then we must do something to help them. If we could be the ideal observers, invisible, unnoticed, then we would have an obligation not to interfere in the slightest. We could gather valid scientific data about them, and if they flourished or perished, were well or ill, tortured or the torturers, we would be the ideal observers, the unseen camera. But we can't be. To make an intimate study, we have to become intimate with them. And that, to me, involves a certain amount of obligation."

"I don't see why we should be obligated to a people who tried to kill us without reason."

"I don't know that they had no reason," Gribardsun said. He turned his large gray eyes on Silverstein, who flushed and chewed savagely on the piece of bison meat he had just put in his mouth.

"I feel I owe some obligations," Gribardsun said. "But I'm not neurotic about it. There are limits to what I owe."

"Are you talking about them or about me?"

"Both."

A little while later he stretched out on a pile of bison hides and apparently went to sleep almost at once. He did not cover himself with furs, as the natives did, since his thermicron suit kept him warm enough. In fact, he had to open some vents in it against getting too warm. The many bodies in the tent built up the temperature.

Silverstein opened his own suit at many places and took refuge beneath three wolf-skin blankets. But he had trouble getting to sleep. The stench of smoke and unwashed bodies and rotting teeth and chamber pots and the loud snoring of the chief and his old mother and a bite now and then from a louse kept him awake for hours. He had no sooner fallen asleep, or so it seemed to him, than a noise awakened him. He sat up and saw Gribardsun pushing the teenager blonde from him. Evidently she had just come over to him. But Gribardsun was having none of her.

In the morning, Drummond commented on the incident. Gribardsun said, "I have no moral objection to temporary matings, and I may even have offended her deeply. She probably wanted to have a child by me because I am a powerful magician and warrior, accord-

ing to her lights. But I would feel an additional obligation if she had a child by me. I'm not ready for any
such thing—yet."

"You mean you may be ready some day?" Drummond queried. "How could that be?"

"You'll know if it happens."

They did not talk much during the rest of the
day except on matters of business. Silverstein filmed
the day's hunting, which consisted of finding a herd of
bison penned inside deep walls of snow. Gribardsun
shot one bull to remind the tribesmen of the power
of his rifle. Then he used spears to kill several more
bulls. After that, he called a halt to the slaughter. By
signs he told them they shouldn't waste the meat by
killing the whole herd. They wouldn't be able to haul
all the meat home today, and if they left carcasses behind, the wolves would get them. The bison were
trapped in the "yard" and most of them would probably starve as soon as they had dug down through the
snow and eaten all the grass under it. This was a common event; the heavy snows often trapped the herbivores.

The next day, Silverstein asked for, and got permis-
sion, to return to home camp. He hesitated a few
seconds before saying, "I don't like to go unarmed."

Gribardsun took the revolver and a box of ammunition from his pack. "Use them with good sense," he
said.

Drummond flushed and said, "Somehow, I have to
clear myself. But I seem to get in deeper all the time.
Yet I swear I'm innocent!"

"You haven't been proved guilty yet," Gribardsun
said. "So you are presumed innocent until then. But
that doesn't mean you're not on trial. The verdict de-
pends on what you do in the future."

"This is the damndest situation!" Drummond said,

striking his thigh with his fist. "Whoever would have thought, when we got into the machine to go to 12,000 B.C., that I would be suspected of trying to murder you? Or that Rachel and I would be estranged, perhaps beyond any chance of reconciliation? This is supposed to be a scientific expedition, but if things continue as they have, we're going to fail! We'll return—if we return—with relatively little to show. And that would be a disaster! If this expedition doesn't pay off, there may never be another. Time travel costs too much!"

"Then I suggest that you curb your emotions and work harder," Gribardsun said. "Now, I prescribe a tranquilizer for you, but not while you're on the way home. You'll need to be as alert as possible.

Drummond agreed to take the pill when he got back to home camp. He also promised to radio the camp every five minutes so his progress could be checked. And he set out across the deep snow.

Silverstein did not get to the Wota'shaimg camp until late that afternoon. Gribardsun received from von Billmann the report that Silverstein had been sighted. Ten minutes later, von Billmann, very excited called in. Silverstein had pulled his revolver as he walked up to Rachel and had shot at her. She had dropped to the ground, and so the bullet missed her. Drummond fired three times as she rolled away but missed each time. By then von Billmann had loosed six rounds from his rifle. One bullet struck Drummond in the left shoulder, spun him around and tore off much of the flesh and part of the bone of the shoulder.

Von Billmann had had a concentrated course in first aid and preventive medicine since he was to take over as doctor if anything happened to Gribardsun. He had slapped pseudoprotein over the wound and then given Drummond massive doses of P-blood from the stores brought from the vessel. Every person in the tribe had been blood-typed, and Gribardsun had convinced them that they could be donors and nobody would establish an evil control over them through their blood. (95% of the tribe was A with 40% Rh negative.)

By the time Gribardsun arrived, late that evening, Drummond seemed to be out of physical danger. But it was evident next morning that he was suffering from more than physical shock. He did not recognize anybody; he seemed to have gone back to the age of twelve. He was a youth on the third level of Budapest, and his mother was dying. He spoke much in Mandarin Chinese, which his mother had taught him. She was half Chinese and had been born in Lin Shiang and lived there thirteen years before her family went to Budapest in one of those massive interchanges of population which took place during the early part of the twenty-first century and still occurred to a lesser extent.

"Here's another obligation for you," Rachel said as she led him into the conical hut.

All Gribardsun could do at that time was to examine him and commend Robert von Billmann for his medical ability.

Since Drummond could not be moved yet, Gribardsun returned in two days to the other tribe, the Shluwg, as they called themselves. He supervised the care of Drummond through the transceiver at various times of the day. The rest of the time, he studied the Shluwg language and also worked out a means of communicating by signs. He succeeded in putting across his intentions and then, leaving them to think things over, he went back to the Wota'shaimg camp. There he performed several operations on Drummond; he replaced the destroyed bone with plastic so that the shoulder would be almost as good as new. When they returned to their time, the plastic could be replaced with bone.

Drummond was sitting up and walking by then. But he was still withdrawn.

The day came when the Shluwg tribe marched into the area next to the Wota'shaimg camp. The Bear People were prepared for this and so, though they were not friendly, they were not hostile either. They did not approve of Gribardsun's idea of amalgamation of the two groups. But they would do as he suggested and try to get along with the strangers.

To do this it was necessary to set up channels for communication and certain rules of behavior. Several people from each tribe were set to the task of learning the language of the other. Gribardsun led hunters from both tribes on a great three-day hunt which brought in an immense amount of meat. He distributed the meat equally and then, after it was prepared, organized a three-day feast. There were only a few fights, which he managed to cut short by threatening to punish both sides severely, regardless of where the fault lay.

Chapter 7

One fine sunny day, the two tribes set off for the trek southward. In three weeks, they had reached Gibraltar. The great rock was larger than in the twenty-first century. Gribardsun halted the tribes long enough to establish contact with several related tribes which lived on or about the rock. Specimens of their language and body tissues were taken along with photographs. Meat was exchanged for their tools and weapons and their necklaces of sea shells.

The blood taken from the Gibraltar tribes was heavily B and slightly A, with four individuals who were O. This presented a puzzling picture. The answer, if it would ever be found, would probably come after all data was brought back to the twenty-first century.

The two tribes marched on across the land bridge which, at that time, was over six miles wide. They entered North Africa and continued along the coast eastward. The coast was about four to five hundred feet below the level of the Mediterranean as the twenty-first century knew it. The group moved slowly, because the three scientists were busy taking specimens and measurements. As the scientific collection increased, more people had to be detailed to carry the growing bulk of information. And that meant that the work of the bearers had to be parceled out among the others. As a result, Gribardsun had to spend more time hunting with the rifle to feed the mob. But he also had to devote extra time to the scientific work, since Silverstein was incapable of performing his duties.

The total range of duties kept Gribardsun working from dawn or before until far past supper. But he was an excellent administrator in that he knew the value of letting his inferiors share the burden.

"I learned that in His Majesty's Service," he told Rachel.

"His? But . . ."

"I meant Her Majesty's, of course."

"Even so," Rachel said, "that would make you born . . ."

"It was just a matter of speaking," he said. "One of the archaic phrases of which I'm so fond. I meant, in the government service, of course. But I learned that if you don't want to kill yourself with work and worry, you delegate responsibility."

"You should be exhausted," she said. "But you look fresh as ever. I'm the one who's dying of overwork and lack of sleep, and yet my duties are as nothing compared to yours."

"You're worried about Drummond."

"Yes. It's all over between us. And he may even have tried to—well, he *did* try to kill me, and I believe he tried to kill you. But he was mentally ill. He couldn't help himself. I don't hate him. I just don't love him any more. Yet, I feel responsible for him. Sorry for him, I suppose. I can understand him. I sometimes feel that I'm going insane myself. I just can't get a strong grip on reality. If this is reality. It all seems so dreamlike and too often nightmarish.

Sometimes I think I'll scream if I don't see something familiar. I know it's blasphemy, from a scientific viewpoint, but I wish that we could return to our time tomorrow. I'd chuck all that has to be learned for a chance to climb aboard and know that in a few minutes I'd be back in the twenty-first century."

"This reaction—this temporal shock—is just as valuable a datum as anything we'll bring back," he said. "I hope it won't cause time travel to be abandoned. I doubt it, since only one of us is very much incapacitated, and we can't prove that that happened because of temporal dislocation. In any event, you can be sure that those chosen for future expeditions will be much more deeply tested. But," he added, smiling, "it will be too late for anybody on this expedition."

"Why do you smile?"

"I'll tell you some day."

The two tribes moved on along the coast of Morocco. Though it was cold, often below freezing, and snow fell, the climate was not as rigorous as in Iberia. They marched more swiftly, but their halts were longer, since the three scientists had enough to do to keep them in each area for six months. The took thousands of photographs, made maps of the coastal areas, took samples of the soil and the water and specimens of flora and fauna, from local bacteria and amoeba and earthworms up to the elephants. They could not take the elephant bodies with them, of course, but Gribardsun and Rachel Silverstein did random dissections and preserved tissue slides. They made Carbon-14 and xenon-argon datings on the spot with their equipment. They fished and then studied specimens before giving them over to the cooks.

The tribes living on the coast were generally small and lived by hunting and fishing. Rivers ran through the Sahara and emptied into the western half of the Mediterranean. The river mouths were plentiful with fish and seal and porpoise, and inland were the elephants and rhinoceroses, antelope and deer and goat, horses, aurochs, and even bison. There were also lions and bears and leopards. Although the great snow leopards existed in France and Iberia, Gribardsun had never seen one in those regions. But he had not been in Africa more than week before he glimpsed three at a distance.

The natives were larger than the Arab-Berber type of the modern era but somewhat smaller, thinner-boned and darker than the modern Europeans. They were also longer-headed and tended toward aquiline faces. So far, no Negroes had been encountered nor had any of the Africans ever heard of black men.

"It's too late, even in 12,000 B.C., to determine the origin of the Negro race," Gribardsun said. "I don't suppose we'll ever know if it's true that they arose somewhere in southern Asia and then migrated to Africa and Austronesia and were killed off or absorbed on the Asiatic mainland. Or if they originated in Africa and then, somehow, some migrated to New Guinea and Melanesia, leaving damn few traces along the trail. Even so, we might learn something if we could explore East Africa now and learn what types are living there. I suspect there'd be some Caucasoid and Capsoid types and perhaps some Negritos."

"You surely aren't thinking of taking us down there?" Rachel said.

"I would object," von Billmann said. "That would take us entirely too far from the vessel; it would definitely imperil the expedition. Moreover, if we're going to roam far and wide, we should be doing it in central Europe, preferably somewhere between the Elbe and

Vistula. We should be ascertaining whether proto-Indio-Hittite speech exists there, or . . ."

Gribardsun smiled but shook his head. "You're the greatest linguist of the twenty-first century, Robert, and you have a very high intelligence. But I have to keep reminding you that those rivers are buried under vast masses of ice. If you ever did find your proto-I-H-speakers, it would be somewhere to the south. Maybe in Italy. Or in France, a few miles from where the vessel emerged. Or maybe on this coast, a few miles ahead of us. Or behind us, a few miles inland."

Von Billmann laughed, but his face was red. "I know," he said. "But that's my blind spot. My brain slips a cog every time I think of my love. I know that glaciers cover that area, but I'm so eager to locate my language, my beloved language, that I forgot. But I have a hunch, an intuition, worthless perhaps and only the expression of a wish, that my speakers are living not too far to the south of the glaciers, perhaps in Czechoslovakia."

"Next year, if circumstances permit, we'll go to Czechoslovakia," Gribardsun said. "We have to study the edges of the glaciers, anyway. And if we can go to North Africa, we can certainly go to central Europe."

Von Billmann had never looked so happy.

The tribes moved on slowly eastward. By now they could communicate fairly well with signs and a mixture of each other's vocabulary. The structure of the two languages was dissimilar, and each contained sounds difficult for a nonnatal speaker to master. The result was the gradual building up of a pidgin. It contained sounds that both the Wota'shaimg and the Shluwg could pronounce, and vocabulary items which the two tribes had agreed to accept, though the agreement was apparently entirely unconscious. The structure of the pidgin tended more toward that of the Wota'shaimg, since they were the dominant tribe. But it was considerably simplified, and before a year was up, its structure had been determined. Von Billmann was ecstatic at being present at the birth of a new language. He recorded it as it developed and, in fact, since he knew more about pidgins and synthetic and artificial languages than anybody in this or any other time, he played a big part in the development of this one. He knew what the ideal language should be, and he used his influence to shape the pidgin.

"If the two tribes stay together," he said, "they may abandon their own language and substitute the pidgin. That would be the most economical and logical course."

Though the two tribes were of somewhat different physical type, and their way of looking at the universe differed greatly in many respects, they shared many similar customs. Their attitudes toward marriage and their sexual habits were near identical, their methods of hunting were identical, and their governmental systems were much alike. They ate practically the same foods; the tabus of each were few, and neither objected to the other tribe eating its tabu animal.

Then Tkant, the big man whom Gribardsun had defeated in the snow arena, decided that he could provide for two families. So he asked for, and got, Neliska, Dubhab's daughter, as his second wife. Gribardsun, as her protector, gave her away. He had one less obligation, though Neliska had asked him, before she accepted Tkant, if he intended to marry her. Gribardsun hesitated and then said that he thought it best if she married Tkant.

Laminak, Neliska's sister, was happy at this decision. She had just gone through her rites of passage and so was, theoretically, eligible at the age of twelve for marriage. In practice, the young females did not marry until they were fourteen; some not until they were sixteen. Most of the early married did not bear children until they were eighteen or even older. This was not because of any method of birth control; the women did not become fertile until relatively late.

On the other hand, some of the tribes along the coast had many females who bore children at the age of twelve. The rate of death at childbirth was higher for both infant and mother in these tribes.

The two tribes walked eastward, encountering peoples who either fled or were easily awed by the display of Very lights or a few shots fired over their heads. No lives were lost on either side in these encounters, and after Gribardsun shot a rhinoceros or two or some wild cattle for the natives, a peaceful if sometimes uneasy relationship was established.

About the middle of January, the group arrived in what would be, someday, Tunisia. Actually, they were in an area that would be underwater off the Tunisian coast in the modern age, but the scientists made a number of treks from their base camp into the interior. Here the snows lay not too deeply over the winter grasses and on top of the many trees. A broad river wound through the land and poured down into the Mediterranean. Gribardsun followed its course for two hundred miles before reluctantly turning back.

"I get the same joy from seeing the vast herds of many different types of animals and the great predators that feed on them as Robert does when he finds a new language," he said to Rachel. "This is the way a world should be. Few human beings, many animals, plenty of water and grass. I would like this even better if there were many more trees, but I know that these do exist further south. The air is pure, and nature works unhindered by man."

"I long for the day when I can return home," she said. "But you sound as if you dread it."

"Far from it," he said. "I look forward with joy to the day that the vessel returns."

That was only one of the many puzzling statements he made. Rachel did not ask him what he meant. By now she knew that he just would not reply.

After a month and a half at their Tunisian camp, Gribardsun gave the word to march again. They set off toward Sicily. The stealing of water by the great northern glaciers had not only resulted in a land bridge across what would be the Straits of Gibraltar. There was another, and far greater, land bridge between Italy, Sicily, Tunisia, and part of Libya. The Mediterranean was, at this time, two smaller seas separated by the extension of Italy.

The tribes moved on the western coast of the bridge with the hills high on their right. And the sixth day out, Drummond found their first human fossil skull.

Apparently, though he was still living in the age of twelve, he had not forgotten everything he had learned since then. He was out walking near the camp, accompanied by Laminak and a juvenile male for protection, when he saw a piece of the skull sticking out of a layer of limestone halfway up a hill.

He told von Billmann of it. He would not speak to Rachel or John then—another indication that he was not entirely stuck at an early age. Robert verified the find and told the other two scientists. They spent a week delicately digging out the skull and some pieces of skeleton and looking for other fossils.

The study of the stratum and the bones, and the gaseous content and decay of the rocks, indicated that the skull belonged to a young man who had lived about 200,000 B.C., during the Third Glacial. His massive features indicated a human intermediate between

Heïdelberg and Neanderthal man. No tools were found in conjunction with the fossil.

The descendant of *Homo heidelbergensis* and the ancestor of *Homo neanderthalensis* was dubbed *Homo silverstein.*

Though every member of the tribe was alerted to evidences of fossils, and some fossil animals and plants were found, no more human fossils were seen.

The land bridge was crossed and the safari was traveling on the west coast of Sicily, or, rather, on land that would be hundreds of feet below the twenty-first century Sicilian beaches. Occasionally, the scientists went to the mountains inland to make observations and collect specimens.

The next bridge was between Sicily and Italy. When they arrived at the mouth of the Tiber, they went up the river valley to the site of Rome-to-be. A small tribe of particularly brutish people lived there. They were short and squat and had skeletal characteristics which indicated a mixing with Neanderthals at some time in the past. They wore no clothes and daubed themselves with mud to keep themselves warm in the winter. Their weapons and tools were far too primitive for even 12,000 B.C., and they practiced cannibalism.

Farther north was another group which was a physical double of the pre-Romans. But these were far more advanced in technology and wore fur clothing skillfully sewn together and used fine stone, wood, and bone tools and weapons. Their language was related to that of the Tiber people.

Gribardsun had a theory that was, he admitted, mystical to some extent, and a modification of Jung's. He believed that each group of people had its own particular *soul* or collective psyche. The factors creating this soul were unconscious but deliberate. That is, the collective mind determined, in some as yet unanalyzable manner, to fashion itself into a mode belligerent or pacifist, lazy or busy, poetic or practical, progressive or static or regressive. Some collective souls yearned for a place by the gods; others, by swine.

The two groups they had just left were examples of the difference of collective psyches in two similar groups. Both had picked up some Neanderthal genes, and isolation from *Homo sapiens* had enabled them to retain these genes. It was possible that the two had only recently been one, and that the split had taken place only a few generations before. But one seemed to be deliberately brutish; the other, quite human.

"I don't think your colleagues at the University of Greater Europe would accept that theory," von Billmann said.

"I do not care. It's only a theory, anyway, with no way to prove it, and I don't intend to waste time trying to do so," Gribardsun said.

By early spring, they had entered that prong of land which took in the islands of Elba, Corsica, and Sardinia. These comprised one land mass connected with Italy and covered with firs and pines and filled with game, including elephants, cave bear and lions. Some of the tribes had Negroid skeletal traits, but they were definitely Caucasoid. Their hair was curly, but only loosely so, and their lips, though full, were not overly everted. There was a small minority of blonds among them.

By late April, the safari crossed the border-to-be between Italy and France. Gribardsun, having determined the border by astronomical and geodesic observations, was the first to walk across the imaginary line. Humming the *Marseillaise,* he strode along. His thick black hair was cut short straight across his forehead; the rest swinging shoulder-length. His face was shaven; he had not yet overcome his dislike of beards. He wore a yellow-brown lion skin cape and a red deer loincloth and brown bearskin boots. The rifle was slung over his shoulder, and he carried a flint-tipped spear in one hand. His big steel hunting knife was in a sheath at his leopard-skin belt.

Behind him came Glamug, holding high at the end of a wooden pole a cave-bear skull. His face and body were painted with bright symbols, and he was chanting a protective ritual. Behind him came the chiefs and chief warriors of both tribes in their pecking order and then the Wota'shaimg. Behind them was the standard bearer of the Shluwg, holding on a pole a wildcat skull, and after him his tribe. The drummers and fluters and whistlers of both tribes were playing their own "national" anthems, and their people were singing, respectively, the Song of the Father Bear and the Song of the Great Wildcat Mother. The only ones whose musical sensibilities were offended were the time travelers.

"Lafayette, we are here!" shouted Gribardsun in French. He seemed to be unusually exuberant that day. They had covered over 3,600 miles in nine months by taking their time at some places and making long forced marches between others. Gribardsun would have liked to stop off for about two weeks to rest at their starting point, the overhang in the Vezeres River valley. After their strength was restored, they could go northwestward across France and cross the land bridge into England, following the Thames, which ran across the bridge and into Europe.

But when, at the end of their two-weeks' rest, he suggested this plan, he found that the tribes refused to go. They had had enough of wandering. Now they wanted to settle down for the summer, hunt animals, pick berries, dig roots, tan skins, fish in the rivers for salmon, hold feasts, repair tents and make new ones.

The chiefs and the doctors looked apprehensive when they said no to Gribardsun. But he did not threaten or shoot off the thunder stick. He replied, smiling, that he understood how very weary they must be and that they had to prepare for the winter in the short time they had. He thanked them for the great endurance and forbearance they had shown in following him around the great waters. It was true that he had shown them many strange lands and peoples and thus broadened their outlook and their knowledge. And he had strengthened them by bringing about the fusion of the two tribes. Nevertheless, they had shown much courage and patience in this great task, and he thanked them.

But he and his colleagues had their work, too. They would leave for a good part of the summer. But they would be back. And he would expect the tribes to be on their best behavior, as they were when he was present. The two tribes must continue to submit any disputes to the council, composed of the elders of each tribe. And they must continue to improve their mutual language, Galush. And they must continue to cooperate in every respect. When he came back he would ask how well the two tribes had behaved toward each other and also among themselves.

If, however, any individuals of either group wished to volunteer to go along with Gribardsun, then they must be allowed to go. He would overrule the tribal elders in this single matter. He needed carriers for the specimens that would be collected.

A number of juveniles volunteered, but their fathers overruled them. They could not be spared. Their absence would impose great hardships on their families.

Gribardsun had to admit that the fathers were right.

In this primitive economy, every able hand must be used to its fullest ability.

The juveniles were disappointed, since they would much rather be roaming around the country than working day and night at home under the strict supervision of father in particular and the tribe in general.

"Very well" John Gribardsun said. "I'll make the trip by myself. I can do it three times as fast by myself. I'll make a flying survey of England as far north as the edge of the glaciers. I think I can do it in four weeks."

Von Billmann said, "Are you running most of the way?"

"Practically," Gribardsun said. "I'll be carrying the rifle and ammunition and a camera and film and some recording balls. I'll live off the country, eat only twice a day, and use every bit of daylight to travel."

"It's about six hundred miles from here to the southern edge of the glacier in England as the crow flies," von Billmann said. "Twelve hundred miles round trip. And you'll probably cover three hundred or so miles in England itself. To get back here in a month, you'll have to average about fifty miles a day."

"I may take a little longer than a month," the Englishman said.

"You won't have any thick woods to slow you up," Rachel said. "But even so . . ."

The night before he was to leave, the four sat around a fire in front of their huts. Most of the tribespeople had gone to bed, filled with meat and berries and boiled greens they had devoured during the feast to celebrate Gribardsun's departure. Many had cried and embraced him, saying that they would miss him very much and hoping that evil spirits or bad animals would not get him. Their grief seemed genuine enough, but Gribardsun remarked later that a sense of relief underlay the sorrow. With him gone, they would be able to get back to a more normal—or at least a less tense—life. Having a demigod around was not conducive to relaxation or comfort.

"I've said that I object to your going off on your own, and I protest again," Rachel said. "You're the one who keeps everybody in line here. Our authority may not be up to keeping the peace between the two tribes. And what if one of us falls sick? You're the doctor. You won't be here to treat us. If something should happen to you—and you must admit that the chances are high—we would have no way of knowing where you are. We couldn't even go looking for you; it would jeopardize the expedition itself. You aren't even taking along a radio."

"As the head of this expedition, I make the decisions," John said. "Everything we do here is chancy. I believe that a survey of conditions in England will be a valuable addition to our data and so the trip is justified. Besides," he added with a smile, "I want to see what jolly old England looks like now. You can't call it a tight little island, of course, since it's just part of a huge land mass extending as far as Iceland. But I am curious to see what the Thames and the site of London-to-be look like. And what my ancestral estates in Derbyshire and Yorkshire look like."

At dawn, Gribardsun stepped out from his hut. He wore a wolf-skin vest and deerskin loincloth and his bearskin boots. He carried a pack on his back containing ammunition and his meager scientific and medical equipment, several containers of dehydrated fruit juice and concentrated protein, a suit and a tent of thermicron (though it was summer it would be cold near the ice fields of England), and a pair of binoculars. He was not even taking shaving equipment, though he could have shaved with the edge of his hunting knife. He was growing a beard on this trip.

Laminak was waiting with the scientists. She threw her arms around him and wept, and he kissed her and told her not to grieve. Rachel looked sour. She had tried to overcome her irrational feelings of jealousy, but she could not endure the child. Gribardsun might seem amused by Laminak's devotion, but she could not get rid of the idea that he was just waiting for her to become a little older. Gribardsun thought so much of her, her intelligence was very high, she was sensitive, perceptive and open-hearted, and showed signs of being a beauty. Before it would be time for the travelers to return, she would be fifteen, and Gribardsun might take her back with him. She believed this despite his protests that that could never happen.

Drummond Silverstein said goodbye to Gribardsun and then burst into tears. He had become very much attached to the Englishman, partly because they spent an hour almost every day in therapy. Gribardsun was using a combination of drugs and hypnotism to break through the wall of time that Drummond had erected inside himself. But he had had little success. However, Drummond had become very dependent on him.

"If I thought that my leaving would injure him, I might stay," Gribardsun said. "But the therapy has not been spectacularly successful, so it won't be upset with my absence. But I want you two to watch him closely for signs of improvement or regression. You have my instructions concerning him."

Ten minutes later, he was out of sight. He left at a trot, which he said he could keep up all day. Except in the roughest terrain, he expected to average about fifty miles a day.

The days passed. The summer was hot but short, and the work for both the scientists and the tribespeople was hard. Rachel trained Drummond to help her in her fields of botany, zoology, and genetics, but had to suppress an ever present irritation with him. She tended to regard him as mentally retarded, whereas he was actually a very bright twelve-year-old. He learned swiftly, but he did make mistakes, and she was sharp with him when these occurred. Nor did she feel sympathetic when he now and then called her "mother." She was, in fact, furious.

Von Billmann showed signs of discontent. More and more he complained about the low chances of ever getting to Czechoslovakia.

"The speakers of proto-Indo-Hittite must be located and their language recorded," he said. "And doing this will take time. We should be traveling there right now. But, instead, John Gribardsun is visiting that barren piece of land, England. I doubt that he'll find a single human being there."

"That's not what he's looking for," she said. "You know he's making a geological and meteorological survey."

"We should have brought along a small plane," he said peevishly. "We could have covered hundreds of miles, saved months of travel time. I could be in Czechoslovakia right now."

She had known von Billmann for many years before the expedition and had never once seen him in a bad humor. Perhaps he was being affected by temporal dislocation. Though he had been more resistant than she or her husband, he was succumbing now. And she, instead of getting better, was feeling less and less attached to reality. She and von Billmann were weakening, she was sure, because their pillar of stability was gone. As long as Gribardsun was around, reality seemed more solid. He radiated strength and assurance.

Chapter 8

A month passed. The hunters brought in hares, lemmings, marmots, voles, grouse, foxes, wolves, ibex, reindeer, horses, musk oxen, aurochs, bison, rhinoceroses, and mammoths. The fishermen brought in salmon and fresh-water mussels. The women brought in berries and tubers and greens of various kinds. Meat and fish were smoked and dried. Tubers were dried or ground into a powder. Skins were tanned, cut, and sewn.

An old man (about sixty) died. Ten babies were born, four of whom died at birth. Three mothers died. A hunter came too close to a mammoth which had fallen into a trap and was lifted up and dashed to death by the huge beast's trunk. A youth fell off a cliff while hunting ibex, broke his back, and was eaten by cave hyenas before his companions could get to him. A man savagely beat his wife when he found her with another man behind a large boulder. She recovered but lost numerous teeth and an eye.

Casualties were normally high among these people, but this month they were unusually high, frighteningly so to the tribespeople. They blamed Gribardsun's absence for the evil things happening to them.

When thirty days had passed, Rachel and von

Billmann began to look for Gribardsun. Every day thereafter they expected, or least hoped, to see his tall, long-legged, broad-shouldered figure and handsome face appear down the valley. But two weeks went by, and they started to worry. They knew that he was not conforming to a timetable, and that he might have run across many interesting phenomena to detain him. But he was a man of his word, and if he said he would be back in a month, he would try to keep reasonably close to that time.

The day of the seventh week after his departure, Rachel was on a herpetological field trip, about five miles from the camp, with Drummond. She had taken films at long range of a field where vipers lived. Having been fortunate to photograph a viper in the act of swallowing a young lemming, she went into the area to catch the snake. She found the hole into which it had disappeared and she and Drummond began digging into it. After fifteen minutes of hard work with the shovel, she exposed the snake sleeping in the burrow with its middle swollen with the lemming. She lifted it and dropped it into a bag.

And then she dropped bag and snake as Drummond yelled behind her.

She whirled and saw him rigid and pointing at a large viper poised to strike only a foot away.

"Stand still!" she said. "And be quiet! I'll get him!"

She withdrew her pistol slowly from her holster, but Drummond yelled again and jumped away as the upper part of the snake's body swayed back and forth. The snake flashed forward at the sudden movement, and Rachel shrieked. She thought that the snake had struck Drummond.

Her revolver missed the viper the first two shots, but the third blew its backbone apart just behind the head.

Drummond remained frozen and grey.

"Did it bite you?" she asked. She reached into the bag she wore suspended from her belt. It held anti-venom drugs, but the effect depended on quick injection.

"I don't think so," he said finally, staring down at his leg. "It struck me, but only with the tip of its snout, I think. I was going away from it when it did hit."

He suddenly sat down and covered his face with his hands. Rachel got down on her knees and rolled up his pants leg. She could find no bite.

"You're all right," she said.

"Where exactly am I?" His eyes looked at her bewildered through his fingers.

She knew then, without being told, what had happened.

"I remember shooting at you," he said. "My God, what happened? Where are we?"

By the time they had returned to camp, he knew everything. But it was all hearsay to him. He remembered nothing from the moment he had tried to kill her.

"And the old snake-pit treatment brought me back," he said. "In one way I wish it hadn't. But of course I wouldn't want to remain a child forever. I wonder why I got stuck at that age? It doesn't matter; I can find out when I get back to our time. If we ever do . . ."

He began to weep, saying as he regained control, "My God, what have I done? What's happened to me? To us?"

She did not reply for a while, and then she said, "Whatever it is, it's something that brought out in us what already existed. It didn't originate anything."

"I can't believe that these psychological changes are brought about just by the shock of time dislocation," he said. "I wonder if there aren't some subtle somatic effects caused by time travel. Something that causes an electrochemical imbalance."

"That is something that will be determined by the medics when we get back," she said. "Unless, of course, the trip back restores our balance."

She started to say something, shut her mouth, then put out her hand to stop him.

"John is gone," she said, "and it's possible he may never return. I can't help feeling that something bad has happened to him. But if he does return, then what? Are we going to go through the same thing? Do I have to be afraid that you'll be shooting at us?"

"I suppose it's all over between us, no matter what I do from now on," he said.

"Yes, I won't lie, even if I am afraid of you," she said. "I'm getting a divorce as soon as we get out of quarantine."

"And then you and Gribardsun will be getting married?"

She laughed and said, "Oh, yes! Right away! You fool! He doesn't love me! I asked him, and he said no!"

"And you two weren't cheating on me? Or intending to?"

"This is the twenty-first century!" she said.

"No, it isn't. It's the hundred and twentieth B.C. You didn't answer my question."

"No, we weren't cheating on you. You know I wouldn't deceive you; I'd tell you what I was doing or what I intended to do. And John would never stoop to do anything behind a person's back. You should know him better than that! Can you actually conceive of him doing anything base or sneaky?"

"Noble John. Nature's aristocrat!"

They were silent. He started toward the camp again but stopped after a few steps.

"I swore I wouldn't ever say anything about this until we returned. But I feel I must tell you now. Only you will have to promise me you won't tell Robert or Gribardsun."

"How can I do that if it turns out that what you're going to tell me may hurt John if I keep silent?"

He shrugged and said, "Unless you promise not to tell anyone, I won't tell you."

Rachel looked steadily at him as if she were trying to tunnel straight into his mind, into the chamber where the secret hid. Then she said, "All right. I promise."

"You mean it?"

"Have I ever lied to you?"

"I don't think so," he said.

He licked his lips.

"Well, here goes. The day before our quarantine, de Longnors called me and asked if he could talk to me in private. You were gone, so I said yes. He was at our apartment in ten minutes, and after making sure the place wasn't bugged, and with me wondering what was going on, he told me everything he knew— and suspected—about Gribardsun."

"Naturally he'd be angry with John."

"There was more to it than that. You see, he'd talked with Moishe, not too long before Moishe died. Moishe was already sick by then, and he knew he was going to die. He called in de Longnors, who at that time was to be head of our expedition. He told de Longnors a strange tale, one which de Longnors found difficult to believe. Moishe said that thirty years before, in 2058, when he was still working on his theory of time mechanics, he was approached by Gribardsun. At that time almost no one knew what Moishe was working on and those who did thought he was a crackpot. In fact, Moishe almost lost his position as an instructor in physics at the University of Greater Europe because his superiors thought he was an imbecile or psychotic. Or both.

"But the pressure from them suddenly and inexplicably eased off. And Moishe was given the go-ahead. Not only that; he was granted leave from his teaching duties and given more computer facilities.

"Moishe said that this took place almost immediately after he had explained to Gribardsun what he was doing. Apparently Gribardsun had a grasp of Moishe's theory that no one else had at that time. Moishe said it wasn't because Gribardsun was such a great mathematician. But he seemed to have an almost intuitive comprehension. As if he spoke—or thought—in a language that had the same structure as Moishe's mathematics. Moishe couldn't explain what his impressions of Gribardsun were, but he felt a repressed force and something slightly *un*human—not *in*human—in him. As if the man had a somewhat non-*Homo sapiens* Weltanschauung.

"Whatever Gribardsun was, he wanted Moishe to go full jets ahead. And Moishe was given everything he asked for. At the time he did not connect the Englishman's visits with what followed. Gribardsun had not promised anything. But later, Moishe made a few investigations—after he became suspicious, that is; he could not prove it, but he suspected that Gribardsun had somehow pulled strings to get the project going. All of this was thirty years before construction on the vessel had started. Twenty-four years before the final project was approved.

"Moishe was always a very busy man. But he got several men interested in Gribardsun, men in the International Criminal Agency who, in the event, took a long time to find out little. But their findings were significant, though unprovable. Mostly, they concluded that something was rotten, not in Denmark, but in England and in Time. And in Africa.

"By using the facilities of the World Reference Bank, they learned that Gribardsun had been interested for a long time in trying to analyze the structure of Time. Moreover, so had his father.

"Now, our John Gribardsun was born in Derbyshire in 2020, which makes him fifty years old—fifty-one by now. He looks as if he's thirty, which is no miracle in this day of rejuvenation drugs. His father, who looked exactly like him, was born in 1980, and disappeared while sailing off the coast of Kenya. Apparently not much was known about his father. Though an English duke, he spent most of his life in East Africa.

"*His* father was born in vague circumstances in West Africa—exact location not known—raised in indeterminate circumstances in West Africa, and came into his ducal title only after some shenanigans on the part of a relative, who tried to bilk him out of it. This man lived most of his life in Africa and then disappeared in 1970, whereupon his grandson became Duke Gribardsun of Pemberley. But the grandfather was born in 1872."

Rachel said, "What about it? What about any of this stuff? What's the point?"

"To start with, from John Gribardsun born in 1872, every Duke Gribardsun spent most of his life in Africa. And though they served their country in war, they took no other part in public life. Moreover, their source of income was very shadowy. They were suspected of having a gold mine somewhere in Central Africa, and the original duke and his descendants had much trouble —if rumors could be believed—with criminals determined to find that mine. And if you think that is a fairy tale, let me tell you that every once in a while an eruption of gold onto the black market could be traced back to Africa. But never directly to the doorstep of the Gribardsuns.

"Money was abandoned everywhere in the early twenties, if you'll remember. The economy of abundance was adopted worldwide. And at the same time the British peerage was abolished. So the Gribardsuns lost both title and their secret wealth at the same time. But our John went into the professions. He was a doctor and also an administrator of the World Reference Bank. He had access to the administrative records, and to the men who kept them, both as their doctor and as their supervisor. A strange double career, don't you think? Especially in these days, when no man has to work if he doesn't care to. Yet Gribardsun had two professions. And during his long and frequent vacations, he spent much time on the Inner Kenyan Sanctuary and the Ugandan Preserve. It was there he did his work for his MQA thesis on physical anthropology. And it was out of there, if you can believe the findings of the ICA, that some strange tales began coming—all about John Gribardsun: his great strength, his ability to live off the jungle, his singular ability to get along with animals. There were even rumors that he was ageless. The natives of the sanctuary and the preserve spoke of that. They claimed that he was several hundred years old and been given a magic potion when he was very young by a native witch doctor. These stories were discounted, of course.

"But then ICA came across some disquieting—or maybe just puzzling—things when they were checking out the World Reference Bank. There were indications—but nothing that could be proved—that the records had been tampered with."

"What in the world are you driving at?" Rachel said. But her eyes were wide, her skin pale, and a pulse beat in the hollow of her neck.

"Well, the ICA men were thorough, and very well trained, but not what you might call imaginative. They put together a picture and then refused to believe it. They did, however, check out the fingerprints, photographs, and biographical data of the John Gribardsun born in 1872 against each of his descendants. They did so, they said, as a matter of routine, but they were looking for something which I don't think they expressed even to each other.

"However, his descendants, though they looked much like him, had different fingerprints. And though the original John never had retinal or ear or brainwave prints, his descendants did. And theirs were unique. But then, false records can be made. And the lives of the later Gribardsun, which should have been much more thoroughly documented and detailed, were almost as shadowy as that of the man born in 1872. The Gribardsuns did not even go to public school; they all had private tutors."

"Curiouser and curiouser," Rachel said, but she did not look as if she were mocking him.

"But the thorough investigation into our John turned up nothing that could be used against him. And so the investigation was dropped.

"But then the first experiments with time travel were made. And that strange block which extended from our time back to around 1870 was discovered. Of all the theories advanced—and there were some wild ones—the wildest was, I believe, the true one. You remember my commenting on it last year when we were talking about the early experiments? Perrault said that perhaps someone who had been born in the late seventies still lived. And the structure of Time was such that no object or person could be sent back to a time when anybody living then was still living in our time. He was scoffed at, of course, because that would mean that somewhere in the world was a man two hundred and some years old."

She nodded and said, "I know. But with the drugs and techniques we now have, some day people will live as long as that—longer—and yet be young."

"Yes, but they didn't have those drugs in the nineteenth or twentieth century."

"Somebody might have. Some backwoods witch doctor perhaps. You can't say it's beyond the bounds of possibility."

He shook his head and hit his temple with the butt of his palm.

"When Moishe heard this theory of Perrault's, he was the only scientist who didn't pooh-pooh it. At least, he made no statement whatever on it. But that 1872 date rang the gong, you might say. He began thinking about Gribardsun. Yet he didn't want to do anything to antagonize the man. Gribardsun, he was sure, was responsible for time travel. He didn't originate the theory or work out the physical techniques, of course. But if it hadn't been for him, Moishe could never have gotten any place. He was certain of that—though, again, he couldn't prove it.

"But what was Gribardsun's motive? If Gribardsun did have the elixir a hundred years or so before anybody else, why was he so interested in time travel, why had he worked so hard to bring it about? Especially when it looked as if he wasn't going to enjoy its benefits. He was only sixth in priority, and he had only gotten that high in some unaccountable manner.

"And then, suddenly, he was second. One thing after another had happened to those in line ahead of him. Sicknesses, a sudden loss of interest or of courage. One man resigned without giving any reasons and took off for Tahiti. Very mysterious.

"Moishe was very sick by this time then. He . . ."

"Are you suggesting that Gribardsun poisoned him, too?" Rachel said.

"No. Moishe was never intended to go on the expedition. He was too old and, besides, he didn't have the qualifications. No, he got one of the rare incurable cancers—as you know—and he was dying. He hoped he'd live long enough to see the expedition off. It was his greatest wish, and he never got it. Moses before the Promised Land, he used to say, when he felt well enough to joke. Which wasn't often.

"But Gribardsun worried him. He couldn't see what sinister motive the man had, if his motive was sinister. Then de Longnors disappeared, and Moishe was certain that Gribardsun was responsible. But Moishe didn't have long to live, and he did owe Gribardsun a great debt, and he did not want to make accusations which would result in the expedition being held up. A few days' delay would mean he'd die before the launching. As it turned out, he did die before the launching.

"Anyway, he told me the story. And he asked me not to tell anybody. But I was to keep an eye on Gribardsun, and, after I returned, if I felt it was justified, I was to reveal the whole story. Of course I promised, but I felt like a fool. The whole thing was so fantastic. Or so I thought then. Now I don't think so at all. And when I get back . . ."

"You still have nothing to tell," she said. "Moreover, you have been mentally sick, and your story would be hushed up to protect you more than John."

"Do you mean that you think it's all nonsense?"

"No, I don't. I think that what you and Moishe suspected is true. But what can any of us do about it? Besides, I can't believe that John would do anything dishonest or in any way evil."

"That's because you're still in love with him!"

"Probably."

Drummond clamped his teeth tightly and balled his hands.

Strange sounds came from beneath his teeth.

Rachel said, "Drummond! Don't! I can't help it! Please don't get sick again! You have to face reality!"

He opened his fists and released the tension on his jaws and breathed out heavily. He said, "All right. I can face it. But I wish . . ."

"There's Robert!" she said. "He looks worried. I wonder if anything's happened to John!"

She ran toward him. Von Billmann said, "Laminak's very sick. I need your help."

The girl was lying on furs on the floor of the tent, the walls of which had been rolled up so that the cooling wind could pass over her. Amaga, her mother, and Abinal, her brother, squatted near her. Glamug was not present with his medicine paint, his spirit-scaring mask, his rattles and bull roarer and his *baton de commandement*. He was out hunting and, since game was scarce near the camp, was probably miles away.

Laminak's skin was flushed but dry, and her fever was 101.6 F. She looked dully at the three as they bent over her, and then she mumbled, "Koorik?"

"He's not here, but I'm sure he soon will be," Rachel said.

She patted the girl's hand, and then lifted her head to give her a drink from her canteen.

With Rachel's help, von Billmann took saliva, skin and blood samples into the little medical analyzer, together with their observations on her fever and other physical symptoms. The analyzer was able to detect every virus and bacterium and germ known to the twenty-first century, to define any type of cancer, and to interpret symptoms.

It took fifteen minutes to run through the samples

from Laminak, and the coded result on the tape was: DISEASE UNKNOWN. POSSIBLE PSYCHOSOMATIC ORIGIN.

Laminak's fever rose to 102.1 F. and stayed there until late that night. She would drink water but had no desire to eat. She became delirious that evening, and she mumbled and groaned much.

Of the few words they could determine, Koorik was the most frequent.

"She's been pining away ever since Koorik left," Amaga said. "Then she brightened up when the time came for him to return. But as the days passed and he did not come, she became sick. Last night, she started to burn, and she will not stop now until she is dead, unless Koorik comes back. And there is not much time for that."

"I can't believe that she could get so sick just grieving for John," Rachel said.

"But she can," von Billmann said. "The tribe has stories of men and women, and children, who have made themselves sick, killed themselves, with grief at the loss or prolonged absence of a loved one. It's a psychological mechanism, true, but it operates far too effectively."

'We don't know that that is the cause of her sickness," Rachel said.

"True. But until we have a better explanation, I'll accept grief."

Rachel stayed with Laminak even after Glamug returned and began to make the camp hideous with his howlings, shrill chantings, rattlings, bull roarings and sudden shrieks. She did all she could to help the girl and at the same time stay out of Glamug's way. She also kept a close observation of the progress of the illness for the expedition's records.

The morning of the third day, just as the sun came up, Laminak breathed her death rattle.

Glamug stopped his shuffling and chanting, got down on his knees, and marked her forehead and breasts with red ochre.

Then he stood up, removed his mask, and looked at Rachel with tired eyes and drooping face.

"For a little while last night, I rested," he said. "And I had a vision. I saw Koorik running toward us across a field with a high cliff ahead. And behind him bounded a lion. The lion was very close, and then Koorik was running through the shallow stream at the base of the cliff. This slowed him down, and the lion roared with triumph, and it seized Koorik. And then they were rolling in the water, and Koorik had only his shining gray knife to defend himself against the great lion. His thunder stick was empty; it had lost its death-dealing powers. And his spear was in the throat of a lioness, the mate of the lion that pursued Koorik."

Rachel understood that Glamug had fallen asleep for a few minutes, though she could have sworn that his racket had gone on all night without a second's break. He had had a dream and, as was the custom, he must tell the nearest person the dream as soon as possible.

"Did Koorik get away from the lion? Or was he . . . ?"

"Was he killed?" Glamug said. "I do not know. The vision faded, and I was sitting outside the tent of Laminak and shivering with the cold. Not with the cold of the night wind, because that was warm. With the cold of the wind that blows death."

Rachel told Drummond and Robert of Glamug's vision. Drummond scoffed at it, saying that it was a wish on the part of the witch doctor, who must resent Gribardsun's takeover of his role as healer. That was all there was to it. Von Billmann, who had experience with sanctuary people, was not so skeptical.

"But if his dream was a form of telepathy, why didn't *I* see John instead of Glamug? I'm much closer to John than that primitive quack!"

"He's no quack; he believes in what he does and practices to the best of his ability," von Billmann said. "As for why he received the message—if there was a message—well, he *is* a receiver, and you are not. He's tuned in, on the proper wave-length."

Rachel sneered, but she was worried. She would have laughed about the vision in her own environment, the towering many-leveled twenty-first century megalopolis, but in this savage world it was as easy to believe in ESP and ghosts as it was to believe in mammoths and cave lions.

It was summer and therefore hot. The huge deer flies and the smaller flies were numerous, and the tribe must not be kept too long from reaping the summer. The wake took place that day, and Laminak was buried at dawn the next morning. A hole five feet long and three feet wide and two feet deep was dug. A mammoth hide was placed in the bottom of the hole and on this bear hides were placed. Laminak, wrapped around the loins with the fur of a female bear cub, her body elsewhere daubed with red ocher, and a chaplet of bright saxifrage around her head, was carried by four men to the grave. There, while drums beat, flutes wailed, and a bull roarer boomed, she was placed on her right side. Her face was toward the rising sun. She wore a strand of sea shells around her neck, and a wooden doll with human hair, the doll she had put aside two years ago but kept with her few valuables, was placed by her side.

More bright saxifrage petals were strewn over her and two mammoth tusks were crossed over her. Then dirt was thrown over her with wooden shovels, and afterward large rocks were piled over the dirt to keep the hyenas and the wolves off.

Rachel wept as the dirt fell over the blue-gray, red-streaked face and the bright yellow hair. She had resented, even disliked the child, because of her love for Gribardsun and his obvious affection for her. But she was crying, and it may have been for both reasons. Even she did not know. But there was no doubt that in the death of the girl she saw more than one death. Perhaps she was reminded of the inevitability of the death of everyone who had been born and who was to be born. Of what use was life when it must end? Once you were dead, it did not matter if you had lived a hundred years, a happy hundred years. You did not know that you had lived, and you might as well never have lived.

Time had discarded Laminak, and Time would remove even the evidences of her burial. Rachel knew every inch of this area, because part of her training for the expedition had been an archeological survey of the territory. Every bit had been dug up, and there was no grave here in Rachel's time. There was not even evidence that Laminak's tribe had camped for generations under this overhang. Sometime in the post-glacial age, storms, heavy rains, and floods would wash away everything from under the overhang down to the time when Neanderthals had lived here. And then the dirt deposited above the Neanderthal layers would be free of human traces. And Laminak's grave would be washed out and her bones carried down the valley and lost somewhere in the river. The waters would come with such force they would roll away even the large stones piled above her.

When the last stone had been placed, Glamug danced nine times around the grave, shaking the baton to the north, east, south and west. Then he abruptly quit the place, walking toward his tent, where his wife had prepared a broth of water and various boiled roots in a bowl made from the skull of a reindeer. He would drink that cleansing drink, and the ceremony would be over.

Two days later, Rachel saw John Gribardsun. She had been filing away the film pellets and specimens in the vessel. Her work completed, she left the vessel and at once saw the tiny figure far to the northwest. Even at that distance, it was obviously John. Using her binoculars, she was able to amplify him enough so that she could see the details of his face. Her heart began beating even more rapidly.

He recognized her and waved at her but did not increase his pace. He was trotting along at a rate that would have prostrated the other scientists and would have left even the strongest of the tribespeople far behind. Yet, when he stopped before her, he was not breathing overly hard.

He smiled and said, "Hello!" and she came to him, put her arms around him, and wept. She told him of Laminak and, with a cruelty she could not understand until later, told him that Laminak had died of grief for him.

Gribardsun pushed her away and said, "You don't really know what killed her, do you? The analyzer isn't infallible or panoramic in its coverage of diseases, you know."

"I'm sorry," she said. "I shouldn't have told you that. But all of us thought that was why she died. It was so evident."

"I can't be bound to one place or to one person," he said. "If what you say it true, then she would have been . . ."

"Unsuitable for you?" she said. "She wouldn't have made a good wife for you after all? John, you must be out of your mind. She couldn't have gone with you to our time. She would have died there, in an alien and completely bewildering world, and cut off from her tribe. If she died just because she thought you would never return, she surely would have died if she were separated forever from her own people. You know how these primitives are."

"I didn't say I planned to marry her," he said. "I was very fond of her. And I feel—I feel . . ."

He turned away and walked around to the other side of the vessel. Rachel wept again, this time partly for her sympathy with him, because she was sure he was crying for Laminak, and partly for herself, because his grief for Laminak meant that he did not love Rachel. Or perhaps her tears were for everybody.

A few minutes later, his eyes red, he reappeared. "Let's go to the camp," he said. "You tell me what's happened while I've been gone."

But Rachel insisted on knowing whether or not he had been attacked by lions. He was surprised, but when she told him of Glamug's vision, he said, "He does have a form of ESP. Nothing too rare in that among preliterates. Yes, I had a run-in with a lion and his mate, and things went much as Glamug said."

"But he said you had only a knife to defend yourself against an unwounded lion."

"That's true," he said. "And here I am, and the lion is dead."

And that was all he would say about the incident.

That night, while his colleagues and the chief men of the two tribes sat around a large fire, he described his journey. He had traveled northwestward on as straight a line as he could maintain. He averaged about fifty miles a day, though there were a few days when he just walked along so that he could make a rapid study of the terrain and the fauna and flora. He had crossed the land that would be under the English Channel when the glaciers had sufficiently melted. He found the Thames and the site of what would be London, much of which was covered with marsh or shallow lakes.

The land was even more barren and tundra-like than in France. He had seen a few mammoths and rhinoceroses, but exceedingly few lions, bears, or hyenas. But there were many wolves, which hunted mostly the reindeer and horses.

He had seen not a single human being, though there should be a few in England along the southern coast.

He journeyed northward and found that the glacier did not cover the site of his ancestral hall between the sites of Chesterfield and Bakewell in Derbyshire-to-be. But it had only recently retreated, and nothing but moss and some azaleas and saxifrage were growing. Gribardsun's other main ancestral holding, in Yorkshire, where his family's twelfth-century castle would stand, was still covered with hundreds of feet of ice.

"I made a number of observations along the glacial front, traveling a hundred miles along it," he said. "And then I turned back and headed toward home. But I was held up for two days in a cave in the land bridge by a pack of wolves who didn't seem to know they should have an instinctive fear of man. There must have been over fifty in the pack; I've never seen such a large one."

"What happened to your rifle?" von Billmann asked.

"I lost it when I was climbing up the hill to get away from the wolves. I was stopping now and then to shoot one, but they were not discouraged by their losses.

They just ate their dead and kept on after me. I think they were especially hungry, otherwise they wouldn't have been so determined.

"Anyway, I slipped and had to grab hold of indentations in the rocks to keep from falling into their mouths. And the rifle went down a fissure, and I could not reach it after I got rid of the wolves. So I went on."

"You should have taken a revolver," Rachel said.

"I wanted as little weight as possible."

"But how did you get rid of the wolves if you had only your knife?" Drummond asked him. Gribardsun had told them that the spear he had used on the lioness had been made after the wolf incident.

"I killed a few as they came up the hill at me," Gribardsun said. "They could only squeeze through the opening into the cave one at a time. After a while, they gave up. I think they'd eaten so many of their own pack, the edge of their hunger was gone."

When told that Drummond had regained his sanity, Gribardsun had made only one comment. He said that he hoped that Drummond had regained all of his mind. Rachel supposed that he meant by that that he hoped Drummond had gotten over his desire to klil her and Gribardsun.

Drummond assured them that he had accepted reality, and that, whatever they did, he would not try any violence. Not that he ever had, except for the time when he had shot at Rachel.

Gribardsun gave Drummond a series of psychological tests designed to uncover deeply hidden feelings of violence toward particular persons. The results seemed to satisfy him, since he gave Drummond firearms. But Rachel noticed that Gribardsun never allowed Drummond to get behind him when he was armed.

Something decisive had happened to that group.

Though there was always a certain amount of reserve among the three—von Billmann alone being treated quite warmly by all the others—they got along with a minimum of friction. All worked harder than before. Moreover, there were long periods when they did not see each other. Their studies of the area around the campsite had exhausted everything of interest there except the tribespeople themselves. They went farther and farther afield on their own specialties.

Winter struck. Though the world temperature was slowly climbing, and the glaciers would melt a little more every year, the cold and the snow were brutal. And this year the tribes had to leave the overhang and follow the reindeer herds. The big game in this area had been cleaned out. Moreover, the herds seemed to have deserted this part of France.

To von Billmann's joy, Gribardsun decided they should head for Czechoslovakia-to-be. They would progress slowly because of the heavy snows, but when they got to Czechoslovakia, they would settle down there for the winter, and also the next summer. Provided, of course, that game was not too scarce there.

They moved north of the Alps, which were covered with giant glaciers, and into Germany and along the Magdalenian Danube—which did not follow the course of the twenty-first century river—and then northward into Czechoslovakia. There they stayed in a semicave during the winter. Thammash, the chief, developed arthritis, which Gribardsun alleviated with medicine. But the medicine had an unexpected and long-hidden side effect, and one day that summer, while Thammash was running after a wounded horse, he dropped dead. Gribardsun dissected him and found that his heart muscles were damaged. The damage was the result of an intricate series of imbalances, a sort of somatic Rube Goldberg mechanism.

No babies or mothers died during birth that year, though there were several miscarriages.

Angrogrim, the strong man, slipped just as he was about to drive a spear into a baby mammoth that had been cut out from the herd. His head struck a rock, and he died even before the baby stepped on his chest and crushed it.

Amaga married Krnal, a Shluwg whose wife had choked on a fishbone.

The following summer, the tribes moved back to the overhang in the valley of Les Vezeres in France. Von Billmann was very disappointed, because he had not found a single language which seemed capable of developing into Indo-Hittite.

"You really didn't think you would, did you?" John said. "Whoever the pre-Indo-Hittites are, they are probably in Asia or Russia somewhere. They won't be migrating to Germany for several thousands of years yet —probably.

"Of course," he added, smiling slightly, "it's possible that they are only a few miles from us at this very moment."

"You have a small sadistic streak in you, John," von Billmann said.

"Perhaps. However, if you are on the next expedition, which will go to 8000 B.C., you may find your long-lost speakers."

"But I want to find them *now!*"

"Perhaps something entirely unforeseen will happen to enlighten you."

Von Billmann remembered that remark much later.

Chapter 9

Time went swiftly, and then suddenly the day of departure was close. Four years had passed. The vessel was crowded with specimens and only a few had yet to be collected. These were mainly spermatozoa and ova which would be taken from animals shot with the anesthetic-bearing missiles. When the vessel returned to the twenty-first century, the frozen sperm and eggs would be thawed out and appropriately united in tubes. The fetuses would be placed in the uteri of foster mothers—cows in the case of most of the larger animals but, in the zoo, elephants or whales in the case of the largest. The biological science of the twenty-first century permitted the young of one species to flourish in the womb of another. And so, the twenty-first century would soon have in their zoos and reservations beasts that had been extinct for many thousands of years.

Moreover, the sperm and eggs of humans were in the cryogenic tanks. These would be united and implanted in human females, and the children would be brought up by their foster parents. In everything except physical structure, they would be twenty-first centurians. But they would be studied by scientists. And their children, hybrids of Magdalenians and modern, would be studied.

To compensate for the mass of the specimens, parts of the vessel had to be removed. Everything was removed except the files and those devices needed to keep the specimens from decay. Everything had been carefully weighed before the vessel was launched, but everything was weighed again. The day before the vessel was to be retrieved, the weighing apparatus was removed, and its mass was replaced with artifacts from thirty tribes, each of which had been weighed.

It was Gribardsun who suggested that each member of the four should also be reweighed.

"If something should happen to one of us, and he wasn't able to get aboard, his weight should be replaced by something valuable."

"For heaven's sake, John!" Rachel said. "What could happen? We're not leaving the vicinity of the vessel except to go to the farewell feast tonight. And if somebody got sick or fell and broke his neck, we'd still take him along."

"True, but I feel that we should take no chances. You know how serious a deviation in weight can be when the tracers'll be searching for us. Let's take no chances whatsoever."

The "reserves," as von Billmann called them, were artifacts reluctantly discarded because there just was not enough room for them. Four piles were carefully selected, each representing the weight of one of the four. Whatever additions or subtractions had to be made were done with mineral specimens.

The celebration that night was long and exhausting and often touching. The tribes, carrying pine torches, followed them to the vessel and then each member of the Wota'shaimg and the Shluwg kissed each of the explorers. And then, wailing and chanting, they retreated to a distance of a hundred yards. There they settled down to wait for the dawn, since the departure retrieval was set for shortly after sunrise.

The four made no attempt to sleep. They sat in their chairs and talked and now and then looked at the screen showing them the outside. The tribespeople were all awake too, except for the babies and small children.

The four talked animatedly and even gaily; for the first time in a long while the shadow of the past had lifted. Rachel found herself hoping that Gribardsun might forget his prejudices against coming between a man and his wife. She would file a divorce claim as soon as she was out of quarantine, and she would convince John that he did love her, that he had only suppressed his love because of his old-fashioned morality.

A few minutes before sunrise, John Gribardsun rose from the chair. He turned, pulled out a black recording ball, and placed it in a depression on the armrest of his chair.

"I'm leaving now," he said. "You'll want to stow my pile of artifacts aboard as quickly as possible to replace my mass. Anything you want to know is in the ball. Please don't ask me anything now or try to hold me back. You can't do that; all three of you together aren't strong enough and you know it.

"I'm sorry to be so abrupt. You're very shocked. But I don't like long goodbyes or arguments, and I knew that that was what I'd get if I told you ahead of time."

He paused, looked at their pale faces, and said, "I'm staying here. I prefer this world to the one we left. That's all."

He turned and pressed the button that opened the vault-like door and stepped outside. As he did so, the tribespeople cried out and some raced toward him. They must have guessed that he had decided to stay with them, and they were happy. At least, most of them were. No man ever lived that was one hundred per cent popular.

Rachel cried out, "Stop him! Stop him!"

"With what?" Drummond said. He had recovered swiftly from his shock and seemed almost as joyous as the tribesmen. "We don't have any guns, and he wouldn't pay any attention to them if we did. And, as he said, he could take all three of us on and not even get up a sweat."

He ran to the pile that was to be Gribardsun's substitute and picked up a bag of artifacts. "You two had better help me, and quick!" he said. "We haven't got much time!"

Rachel was weeping by now and she looked as if she would like to run after Gribardsun. But she picked up a bag, too, and walked to the vessel after Drummond. Von Billmann followed her with two sacks. He lowered them to the floor by the entrance and blocked her as she tried to get out again. Drummond pressed the button, and all three were quickly shut in again. They got into their chairs and strapped themselves in and waited.

On the screen they could see Gribardsun standing before the tribe. He lifted a hand in farewell.

Sixty-three seconds passed. And they were back in the twenty-first century. The vessel was forty yards from the edge of the hill, and the walls around the buildings of the project towered over them. Then figures clad in white helmets and suits, carrying tanks on their backs and hoses in their hands, stepped out of a small building to their right. The first phase of the quarantine had started.

Von Billmann answered the chief administrator. The eyes of the entire world were on them; every-one of the nine thousand, nine hundred and ninety-nine channels were devoted to the time vessel. But Rachel was paying no attention to the outside. She had dropped the recording ball, no larger than a child's marble, into the machine, and she was listening to John Gribardsun's voice.

Seven days later, the three were allowed to leave. The first thing they did was to go to the valley below, where the overhang still existed. Here they saw the hole in the back wall, broken open by the archeologists and project scientists. Behind six feet of rock was the chamber Gribardsun had promised they would find. And they also found the great stacks of artifacts and records that he said he planned to leave there, if he lived long enough.

Most of the recordings were in the form of John's handwriting on vellum and then on paper. But his last message, made in 1872, was recorded in a ball in one of the machines he had taken from the vessel.

"To you three, Robert, Drummond, and Rachel, it's only been a week, but to me, almost 14,000 years have passed. I have lived for more than that; I have lived far longer than seems right.

"I did not think, the day I said goodbye forever to you, that I would live nearly this long. I am completely unafraid of death—which makes me somewhat non-human. I'm not afraid—but I also have a very strong will to live. Yet, the mathematical probabilities of my living this long were very low. So many accidents can happen in 14,000 years; so many people and beasts would try to kill me. But they failed, and though I came near dying a number of times, I still live.

"I still live. But for how long? Today is January 31, a Wednesday.

"Tomorrow, or sometime in the next few days, I'll be conceived.

"Will Time tolerate two John Gribardsuns?

"Is there something in the structure of Time which will kill me? Or will I be erased from the fabric of Space-Time?

"I'll know only if I am spared. If I am killed or erased, I will be conscious one second and unconscious, because dead or obliterated, the next.

"Whatever happens, I can't complain. I have lived as no other man has lived, and for longer than any other man has lived.

"As you know now, I was fortunate enough to be given an elixir by a witch doctor who was the last man of his tribe. He belonged to a family the original head of which, some generations before, had discovered how to make the elixir, a vile-tasting devil's brew, from certain African herbs, blood, and several other constituents I will not even hint at. He had a high regard for me because I saved his life and also because he thought I was some sort of a demigod. He knew of my rather peculiar upbringing.

"But all that was explained on the ball I gave Rachel.

"How are you, Rachel? And you, Drummond? And you, Robert?

"Strange to speak to the unborn. I have gotten accustomed to speaking with the long dead. But the unborn—Well, I won't take up the valuable recording space in the ball to talk about the paradoxes of Time. That could go on and on.

"Robert, I know that the expedition of 8000 B.C. located your pre-Indo-Hittite speakers. I was one of the informants. None of the expedition suspected that I had already recorded the pre-I-H dialects in far more detail than they would ever be able to do with their limited time. And they were looking for me, too. I suppose they were looking for me because of this message. But they failed. I won't tell you why, of course, because then the expedition would be able to identify me. Even if, in a sense, the expedition has already occurred. Well, I said I'd not get into the paradoxes.

"You'll find, Robert, that your pre-Indo-Hittite speech of 8000 B.C. arose from the very last place you would have suspected.

"Our two tribes, the Wota'shaimg and the Shluwg, eventually abandoned their original tongues and adopted the pidgin. The result was a simple analytical system. But over the course of six millennia, it became a polysyllabled synthetic speech which eventually developed into the pre-Indo-Hittite the second expedition studied. And this, of course, became the Germanic, Balto-Slavic, Indo-Iranian, Greek, Italic, Celtic, and a dozen other language families which were not recorded or even heard of by civilized peoples. Until now."

Gribardsun chuckled and said, "So if it hadn't been for time travel, Robert, Indo-Hittite, and hence, German, Yiddish, English, French, and all those other related tongues would never have existed.

"Yes, I know you're going to say that our tribes had different blood groups than the Indo-Hittite speakers. But many invasions—migrations, rather—occurred from the East, and our tribe, which had become rather large between 12,000 B.C. and 8000 B.C., absorbed so many of the newcomers, and imposed their language on so many, that the original blood group was largely lost."

Von Billmann had turned pale shortly after Gribardsun started talking. He sat down. He seemed to be having trouble getting his breath. Rachel brought him a drink of water, and he sat up and looked around as if he hoped someone had strength to give him.

"Do you realize what he's saying? I won't be on the

8000 B.C. expedition! But why? Was I dead before it could be launched? Or—why?"

Anderson, the project head, turned on the recorder again, since no one could give an answer and they did not want to dwell on the subject.

"There was one other expedition, that which was sent in 3500 B.C. to the Mesopotamian area. The others that had been planned were not realized. I waited for them, but they did not show. I wonder why. Something catastrophic prevented them? I don't know, and you, of course, won't know why until it happens.

"Be that as it may, here are the collections I made. The expedition would never have been made if it had not been for me, as you now know. But I still feel a sense of obligation to the people who gave me this chance to live when the world was fresh. And I have had so much scientific training that I do appreciate what this collection will mean. So, throughout the millennia, I have cached artifacts and specimens and made notes. There are at least a hundred thousand photographs here, since I kept back some of the balls for this purpose. You will find photographs, surreptitiously taken, of course, of the original historical Hercules—myself—Nebuchadnezzar, the historical Moses—not myself—Julius Caesar, Shakespeare, Eric the Red, whom I took from behind a bush, having been waiting for six months for him to land, the historical Odysseus, the real city of Troy, the first Pharaoh, several of the first emperors of China and Kublai Khan and Marco Polo. There are also photos of the historical Jesus, Gautama, and Mohammed, Charlemagne, Saladin, the historical Beowulf, a group photograph of the actual founders of the city of Rome. No Romulus and Remus existed, I am sorry to say.

"I could go on, but you'll find everything catalogued.

"I was a merchant-ship captain supplying the Achaean army, and I am mentioned in Homer, though not exactly in the role of a merchant. But I stayed away from the fighting there, as I stayed away from most fighting. As I stayed away from most centers of civilization. I decided that if I was going to survive for a long time, I would have to live a backwoods, back-country life. I spent altogether a thousand years in the wilds of Africa and another in Asia and the pre-Columbian Americas, though not in a continuous stretch, of course.

"Still, I got hungry for city life now and then, and I did want to keep watch on the rise of civilization. So I spent time in Egypt and Mesopotamia and along the Indus and the Yellow River and in ancient Crete and Greece. And I was once Quetzalcoatl, the details of whose story you will find here.

"I have been everywhere a dozen times and seen everything. I was the first human to set foot on the island of Tahiti; the second time I went there, I beat the first raftload of Polynesians by a week.

"But all this is in the records.

"I have been married many times and fathered many children. Each of you is my descendant. I would say that almost every human being that has lived since 5000 B.C. is my descendant. I am my own ancestor many times over.

"I could talk forever. I could reveal what lay behind many of the great mysteries of history and I could solve many of the lesser, but just as intriguing, mysteries. For example, I was on the *Marie Celeste*.

"I will be sitting under this overhang when my moment of conception comes. What will happen then? I suggest you researchers read the newspaper accounts and determine if the body of a man six-foot-three, with black hair and gray eyes, was found on this ledge. If it wasn't, then I may just have disappeared. Or perhaps I was found only after I'd become a skeleton. Or some body snatcher took me away. The possibilities within Time's fold are many.

"Whatever happens, I am grateful that I have lived a life such as no man has lived.

"And now, Rachel, for you. You will be on the 3500 B.C. expedition. And we will be married in Ur of the Chaldees. You will decide to stay behind when your colleagues return to their time.

"And there we two will live as Terah and his wife, and you will bear Abraham.

"I tell you this because, of course, the time came when we had to part again. You never got the elixir because I never had a chance to analyze it and so make some more. So you died.

"I am telling you this so that you may try to change the course of Time. If you decide not to go on the expedition, then something will happen contrary to my experience, to my knowledge of Time as it happened.

"Is this possible? I don't know. I'll know the day the expedition arrives.

"But I did come to love you, Rachel. And you were the ancestress of Moses and King David and, of course, of yourself. And of me.

"But perhaps you do not want this.

"We shall see.

"In the meantime, here is my collection, the secrets of the ages revealed, art objects that were thought lost forever. Knowledge that mankind would never have possessed otherwise.

"Time's last gift.

"Goodbye, my friends. Hello, Rachel. Perhaps."
There was an uproar when the voice ceased.
Rachel was weeping.
But she was happy.

NOTABLE SELECTIONS FROM THE PUBLISHER
OF THE BEST SCIENCE FICTION IN THE WORLD